"What a wonderful piece of writing! What an exhilarating adventure! What a madcap exploration of mushrooms, paintings, Rimbaud, the legend of Orpheus, and the mazes of a poet's mind, in a jigsaw puzzle of a book that ultimately (like Alice's Wonderland) makes absolute sense!"

—**Alberto Manguel,** author of *The Library at Night* and *Fabulous Monsters: Dracula, Alice, Superman, and Other Literary Friends*

"An immensely pleasurable read."

—**Pascal Quignard,** Prix Goncourt award–winning author of *The Roving Shadows*

"In this book oblivion is daylight."

—**Éric Vuillard,** Prix Goncourt award-winning author of *The Order of the Day*

"A book filled to the gills with a veritable feast of literary ingredients. To read *Aseroë* is to experience a kind of inebriation as we drink in the intelligence and the talent of its author."

—**Marie Étienne,** *La Quinzaine Littéraire*

"Ranging from the mysterious mushroom known by the name of *Aseroë* to Giorgione's painting *The Tempest*, while meditating on the millions made off the work of Rimbaud, [*Aseroë*] offers a series of astonishing and detailed variations on the theme of the figures of forgetfulness."

—**Claire Devarieux,** *Libération*

Aseroë

François Dominique

TRANSLATED BY
Richard Sieburth
AND
Howard Limoli

Bellevue Literary Press
NEW YORK

First published in the United States in 2020
by Bellevue Literary Press, New York

For information, contact:
Bellevue Literary Press
90 Broad Street
Suite 2100
New York, NY 10004
www.blpress.org

Aseroë was originally published in French in 1992 as *Aséroé* by POL éditeur
Text © 1992 by François Dominique
© POL éditeur
Translation © 2020 by Richard Sieburth and Howard Limoli

Library of Congress Cataloging-in-Publication Data
TK

Bellevue Literary Press would like to thank all its generous donors—individuals
and foundations—for their support.

 This publication is made possible by the New York State
Council on the Arts with the support of Governor Andrew
M. Cuomo and the New York State Legislature.

NATIONAL ENDOWMENT FOR THE ARTS This project is supported in part by an award from
the National Endowment for the Arts.

Book design and composition by Mulberry Tree Press, Inc.

Bellevue Literary Press is committed to ecological stewardship in our book
production practices, working to reduce our impact on the natural environment.

♾ This book is printed on acid-free paper.

Manufactured in the United States of America
First Edition

1 3 5 7 9 8 6 4 2

paperback ISBN: 978-1-942658-78-8
ebook ISBN: 978-1-942658-79-5

To Suzanne Limoli
and Richard Sieburth

1

Aseroë

S HE HAS ALWAYS AROUSED special feelings in me. Every year, at the outset of summer or sometimes as late as mid-autumn, I never fail to pay her a visit. It doesn't take me long. While others might pass within a few feet of her, I see her from a distance, I recognize her, I approach her and bend down over her and in a soft voice speak the words that suit her, the name she bears. She immediately starts to blush. Her slender, elegant foot—as with all her kind—is attractively flushed.

I have no illusions: I know this slight flush is not a response to any affectionate words I might address to her, but a reaction to the properties of the ambient air, to the amount of carbon dioxide that the natural respiration of plants (or just my tainted breath) is likely to increase.

Once picked, she takes on a more vivid coloring, as though indisposed. She'll be just as sweet to the taste, crisp and scented, so long as you don't spoil her aroma with garlic and spices or smother her in common meadow mushrooms.

Amanita rubescens is the only apparently sentient mushroom I can name.

People are right to avoid that very ancient but very foolish tendency to project human attributes onto nature. I stroll through the woods, overwhelmed by the scenery—the dawn's light, the lofty peaks, the crystal springs—and my mind is stupefied by the flood of metaphors that invade me.

Determined not to dabble in tawdry imagery, I wondered whether a state of mind might exist—or rather, a state of matter—in which words and things were not separate. If so, this discovery would open up a radically new field to all the forms of creation. As I idly posed to myself this curious question, I couldn't begin to suspect the inhuman character of the artificial reality that would inevitably ensue.

I think the moment has come to explain my

experiment. Let me first point out that mushrooms make up a very vast and almost infinite collection. When experts suggest the figure of 120,000 species of mushrooms, they know this figure has to be increased over the course of years: the multiplication of varieties, the abrupt mutations, the disclosure of new forms whose spores have been lying dormant for centuries force us to add endlessly to the matrix of a rigorous classification system already encumbered with unclassifiable types as well as with strange subspecies and their offspring. Besides, certain of these mycological abortions are so odd that you wonder whether the classification system itself, so patiently worked out by Quélet, Kühner, Pilát, Romagnesi and so many others, shouldn't be reopened for examination.

What animal or vegetable species would be capable of evolving to the point of rendering obsolete the great divisions between vertebrates and invertebrates, cryptogams and phanerogams? Not a single one. That doesn't prevent the animal or vegetable kingdom from creating new species (the innumerable varieties of orchids provide a good example), but in these cases the main lines of the classification system have reached a sufficient level of certainty to embrace all species, including those whose lives—yet to come—cannot be named.

As for mushrooms, it's another matter altogether. They don't belong to a defined kingdom. In a number of ways, they are animals, protozoans or protophytes; in other ways, they're vegetables whose growth is geotropic, like certain algae. Since their appearance on Earth seems to have preceded both the vegetable and animal kingdoms, people simply say that they share properties with both. Consequently, it will take, among all the subspecies yet to come, only a single mushroom whose properties clearly belong both to the animal and vegetable worlds for the great division between Basidiomycota and Ascomycota to collapse on the spot.

I would have preferred my experiment to deal with the family of mushrooms called Amanitaceae fungi. They are elegant, finely colored, and always display—except for the fly agaric, or *muscaria*—a certain propensity toward solitude, which appeals to me. In addition, *Amanita* seem to want to behave as if they provide the most significant illustration of those problems that the life of silence and the power of naming share: gentleness and violence, good and evil, edible and nonedible, fertile and murderous. In this they resemble that "good/bad" thing that Plato submits to the hasty judgment of the young Alcibiades. Yet from the point of view of beauty, they escape contradiction: they are all splendid, without exception. The most beautiful and finest of them all (preferable to the morel and the truffle) is the *Amanita* of the Caesars, or True Orange, whose color evokes the fiery opal (first comparison), the sun's disk at twilight (second comparison), or the mineral arsenic (number three). At the opposite extreme (but no less beautiful, all white and nacreous) is the *Amanita phalloides* (or death cap mushroom)—poison to the core. Horrible abdominal pains, profuse sweating, a burning thirst, shivering, cramps, progressive cooling of the extremities accompanied by terrible anxiety: such are the harbingers of the death, one to three weeks later, of any enemy who might eat it.

Thus, two varieties of the same genus—the *Amanita*—offer the best and the worst. The mind is the only thing I can name that shares in such extremes.

But I needed to find a different species, less fixed, more capable of abrupt mutations, which might *simultaneously* modify the order of things and the system of naming them.

❖

There is another type of mushroom, almost bastardized, an ill-defined member of the family of Phallaceae, which the experts have named *Anthurus archeri* and which occurs in the form of *Aseroë*.

Having originated in Tasmania and South Africa, it appeared in France very suddenly in the fall of 1920, in the environs of La Petite-Raon, to the south of Saint-Dié on the western slope of the Vosges Mountains. One finds in the press of that period reports of a superstitious nature and accusations of witchcraft leading to investigations by the police. These new forms of *Anthurus*, which appeared so abruptly in the underbrush of the Vosges Mountains, were a definite cause for alarm. One doctor in Saint-Dié, named Lucas, went so far as to declare that this unknown fungus was a carrier of infectious germs introduced into French territory by German patriot extremists seeking their postwar revenge. An epidemic of flu over the course of the winter came just in time to back up his claim and to furnish a few certified lunatics with the basis for a legal action to be taken against the military authorities (*Journal des Vosges*, October 26, 1920, p. 3).

Today the *Anthurus* has become common in Burgundy (near Cîteaux Abbey), in the Jura Mountains, and in Savoy. It should take only one or two generations for it to reach all the forests in Europe.

The *Anthurus archeri* initially assumes the form of a round, firm, membranous egg. If one cuts it open, one observes in either half, embedded in its translucid and cartilaginous flesh, two ruddy structures whose curvature and folds evoke a twinned fetus in its first stage of gestation, before any part of it has acquired the contours allowing for more precise identification. After several days, the cuticle cracks, allowing for the emergence of between five and seven thinly drawn triangular lashes, which rapidly sprout from the earth and rise up to six or eight inches above the surface of the soil, then curve backward like iris petals. These lashes have a scarlet surface, covered with a coarse gleba. Several days later, the gleba becomes covered with a network of damp black pustules.

From the beginning of this strange flowering, the fungus emits an odor so unbearable and so persistent that even the most distracted passerby cannot fail to notice it.

Arrived at their full maturity, the most beautiful of these specimens resemble fingers or, rather, the talons of a raptor curled earthward. I know of no other animal that has a skin so obscene. The thing looks like a flayed cadaver, immobile, anchored to the earth.

❀

Having just written all this, I stand back to assess the negative effects of my experiment. In order to report on a new form of life, I wanted to avoid the weight of metaphor, but far removed from the realm of living things, I realize I have given in to mere imagery. I had thought that this most singular of all mushrooms, given its unique character, might have allowed me to avoid the pitfalls of figurative language, yet it relentlessly confounded my thinking and propelled me into the improper use of zoomorphic and anthropomorphic imagery—that is, "egg," "flesh," "members," "skin," "fingers," not to mention the unavoidable "flayed cadaver" of the dissection table.

For me, this business is more serious than it seems. It has taught me, at considerable cost, that one has to submit to the unruliness of metaphorical description in order to gain access to another level of perception and of language, to another form of life.

To make myself clear, let me point out that the vocabulary of mycology (in whatever language) insidiously invites organic, libidinous metaphorization. There is no perversion, even the most morbid and the most criminal, that remains unsuggested by even the most learned and objective of mycological descriptions. I have now come to realize that this particularity, which is without any example in the other natural sciences, does not depend on the native language or on the prurient turn of mind of the specialist; it stems from the thing itself, from the fundamental character of all types of mushrooms.

I could prove this assertion by a detailed analysis of the Latin binomials that form the basis of the terminology of mycology, but a list of common names, better known to the reader, should be clear enough. Here they are in French:

> *Unguline marginée, vulvaire gluante, vesse-de-loup, trompette-des-morts, tricholome malpropre, tremellodon gélatineux, tête de Méduse, sulfurin puant, satyre puant, striée hirsute, entolome livide, pied de griffon, phallus impudique, oeuf du diable, oignon de loup, nymphe des montagnes, nonnette voilée, mucidule visqueuse, marasme brûlant, lépiote déguenillée, langue de chat, lactaire languissant, grosse queue, gorge noire, flammule pénétrante, exidie glanduleuse, drosophile larmoyante, doigt de gant, cul rouge, cul vert, bise de curé, amanites étranglées, engainées, phalloïdes, vaginées, vraies et fausses panthères, agaric meurtrier.*

And here, in English translation:

> *Marginated claw, sticky vulva, wolf's fart, trump of the dead, filthy gland, tremulous jelly, Medusa's head, stinky sulfur, stinky satyr, hairy groove, livid embryo, griffon's foot, shameless phallus, devil's egg, wolf's onion, mountain nymph, veiled novice, slimy milkcap, burning marasmus, unspooled scurf, cat's tongue, languid lacteal, lewd tail, black breast, penetrating flamelet, glandular surge, teary flycatcher, glove finger, red butt, green butt, priest's kiss, strangulated, sheathed amanta, phalloids, vaginateds, true and false panthers, deadly agaric.*

I have, unfortunately, every reason to believe in the *reifying* power of certain words that have no other use in ordinary life than to arouse the senses and thus merely lead the flesh to orgasm or disgust.

Sed occurrit quiddam de nihilo.
Nam ex quocumque fit aliquid, id
causa est ejus quod ex se fit, et omnis
causa necesse est aliquod ad essentiam
effecti praebat adjumentum. (Anselm
of Canterbury, *Monologion*, 8, 1). It
goes without saying: no sooner said
than done.

Whoever has made their way through the
underbrush in the fall can observe, without,
however, being able to explain the fact, that
mushrooms exert a power of attraction over language. Indeed, whether picked or not, they have
this strange capacity of transmitting a little of
their indeterminate substance into the words that
everyone adorns them with; so that one must
wonder, long after one has left them behind,
whether they don't leave some trace of their existence upon our actions as we tend to our daily
lives, far from the woods.

Could it be that this oldest kingdom of nature
among living things has transmitted to succeeding kingdoms (vegetable, animal, and human)
the privilege of here and there arousing a muted

organic presence, a substantial manifestation of the passage from the inert to the living—of which the mind, a latecomer, has retained only an unconscious trace and about which it can say nothing?

Hence, this uncanny power of attraction that exists between the word and *this thing*, this fungus among us, both situated at the two extremes of evolution, whenever they happen to meet.

❖

On October 13, I resolved to test this hypothesis by taking on the Phallaceae whose resemblance to the reproductive organs of the human race can escape only the most nearsighted or the most benighted of creatures.

The mycological classification system provides an "analytical key" permitting specialists to identify an elusive species more rigorously than by the comparative use of a photograph or a drawing. Thus, all known mushrooms can be described in accordance with their perceptible characteristics (odor, texture, appearance, color, spore shape, reaction to certain chemicals) that pertain to a genus or to a more restricted class, to a family, a species, a subspecies, down to the precise identification, by successive eliminations, of the elusive specimen in question.

If I consider *Anthurus archeri*, the "octopus stinkhorn" or the "devil's fingers," I can identify it by noting, in turn, the characteristics of its division (Basidiomycota), of its class (Agaricomycetes), of its order (Phallales), of its family (Phallaceae), of its genus (*Clathrus*), and then of its species.

The Phallaceae include a small number of genuses and species: *Phallus impudicus* (that nauseating cone sometimes called "devil's egg"), *Mutinus caninus* (or "dog stinkhorn"), *Clathrus ruber* (or "basket stinkhorn," a kind of latticed sphere, partially open, like an enigma), *Colus hirudinosis* (another absolutely repulsive stinkhorn fungus), and *Anthurus archeri*.

Not much is known about the propagation of Phallaceae; they disappear here, appear elsewhere, thousands of kilometers away, and clearly adapt to the local climate.

I decided to sleuth out *Anthurus*, watching for the slightest mutation, and, if possible, the appearance of a new species, as yet *unnamed*. If my experiment were to succeed, I would find myself faced with the following alternatives: either the discovery of a new Phallaceae and the invention of an appropriate name or the naming of an unknown species, which, ipso facto, would cause it to materialize.

The first procedure is the one used by the researcher. It was recommended by Jehovah in the Garden of Eden (Gen. 2:19), even though the creation story never breathed a word about mushrooms.

The second procedure is a matter for jack-asses, obscurantists, Jehovah Himself, poets, or misunderstood experts. I was tempted by this second one, without having the presumptuous-ness of including myself in any of the categories cited above. I had to proceed as I saw fit, in order to throw light on the strange relationship that mushrooms maintain with the world of thought.

I returned to the same place several days in a row, in the forest of Cîteaux, after having noted, between the arbor and a group of dogwood trees, lodged on a dark, broken surface, a form of *Anthurus archeri*. On the preceding night, its eggs had ripped through the layer of dead leaves. The soil was lukewarm. In spite of the abundance of very common species such as the peppery *Lactarius*, the *Anthurus* was growing alone, isolated from every living creature around it.

Despite the mushrooms' obnoxious odor, I bent over the soil and cried out to several large specimens that had reached maturity: *Anthurus archeri*! *Anthurus aseroë*! I couldn't stay long in that bent-over position—not because of the smell, but because I felt ridiculous. I looked around; then I returned to the same spot, but without bending over or uttering a word. Nothing happened.

❃

All week long, I made my way to the site of the experiment in the dawn light. I saw the *Anthurus* droop, its pseudopetals (more and more ravaged and pustulant) detaching themselves from the bulb, drying up, and rotting. At the point where the most hardy specimens seemed on the verge of disappearance, already mingled with the mulch of dead leaves, I caught myself mechanically pronouncing *"Anthurus archeri sensu Dominici."* I immediately tried to get hold of myself and to supply the correct name: *Anthurus archeri.* I wouldn't have had the right to add *sensu Dominici* unless I had myself discovered a subspecies of *Anthurus* or even a new characteristic of the old species, a simple detail that might have escaped the experts until then. Meanwhile, I repeated *"sensu Dominici."* I think I'm alert enough to avoid any error in observation; I am leery of the hermeneutic delirium that leads certain learned scholars to devote hundreds of pages to a bagatelle. No, I had to admit it: my faculties were not deceiving me. I was witness, in my innermost being and against my will, to a proliferation of names provoked by the mere presence of *Anthurus archeri.* Its precarious life, at the point of vanishing, was clinging to my tongue, to my bumbling thought. I could hear myself reciting a stream of terms including French, Latin, and Greek words, as well as words pouring in from other languages unknown to me.

I made my escape, and the pentecostal phenomenon of which I was the victim ceased. I stopped going to this wood until the end of autumn. But this flight wasn't enough to protect me from a serious infection. During the week following my experiment in involuntary *verbigeration*, I caught myself, early one morning, copying down into a notebook lists of names that seemed to be the names of Phallaceae. In less than three days, I had written down more than 120 species, in addition to the five species recognized by Romagnesi's analytical key. At that rate, I could have had more than six hundred new species to my credit before mid-November.

❖

This period was a nightmare. To blacken page after page with newly coined words could only be a meaningless exercise, whether in the service of poetry or the natural sciences. But I persevered, despite myself, in this distressing task. That's when I considered putting an end to my days, be it out of cowardice or out of the fear of the unknown.

On November 11, I got up painfully, my mind worn out by this uncontrollable proliferation of newly named mushrooms. The fungi kept coming and coming. . . . I had covered endless notepads and notebooks with my crabbed handwriting.

I had been avoiding going out for a week. Even the sight of my garden through my window had become unbearable; I feared that nature would answer my summons in some insane way.

If the proliferation of new genuses rendered Romagnesi's classification system useless, I could see the time coming when entire genuses that were universally loved, such as the *Boletus* or the *Tricholoma*, would be driven out of existence by this invasion of names without things.

Early that November morning, there I was in the woods, ready to do whatever it took to put an end to this torture. I approached, empty-handed, the location of the experiment. I bit my lips so hard that I drew blood, trying not to say a thing. The ground was bare. Where the *Anthurus archeri* had stood, the rotted leaves had broken down into a black mulch. A few straws, swept by the wind, were scattered here and there. I bent over the soil and, without waiting for the parasitic words to spill in chaotic fashion from my mouth, shouted out at the top of my lungs, then called out softly, "Come here . . . close to me. . . . Don't be afraid. . . . I won't hurt you."

Then, seeing the earth stirred by a slight breeze, I bent forward and, gluing my lips to the cold surface of the ground, vomited up the whole list of names.

❈

As evening approached, I returned to my home, exhausted. I felt a great tenderness for the garden and the house. New forms of *Aseroë* were growing along my walls, like common dandelions. The weather was beautiful; the sun wavered in the dusk.

I wasn't sure if night would fall.

2

Aseroë

I CAN'T GET OUT OF MY MIND what this simple word, *Aseroë*, has cost me in terms of risk and ✳ peril, of danger and exhaustion.

On September 20, somebody, thinking to please me, sent me a few sentences copied from a book:

> *For sale, bodies and voices, for sale,*
> *enormous and unquestionable riches,*
> *for sale, that which will never be sold*
> *. . . The salesmen have not run out of*
> *their stock! It will be some time before*
> *travelers have to submit their invoices.*

Before approaching—I can already feel it—this forbidden zone, I hand over to the idolaters of little Arthur, to the zealots of the Grand Seer, to the Rimbaud Maniacs, to the street-corner Illuminati, to the worshippers of holes without rims and underlined silences, these random reflections of a purely inventorial nature:

Names	Number of Camels
Saïd Massa	5
Abd el-Kader Daoud	12
Moussa and Sanzogoda	19½
Hassan Abou Boku	1½
Djabem	1
Ali Abey	10½
Assorted People of Tadoujna	12½
Saddik Hoummedan	5
Omar Bouda	3½
Mohammed Kassem and Abou Beker Balla	4½
Boguis	1½
Bouha	1
Hoummedou and the Adaïels	13
Total:	**90½**

While some well-meaning friends were agitating, unbeknownst to the young Rimbaud, for the publication of his *Illuminations*, the poet was busying himself with the Labatut caravan account books, finally set up in the fall of 1887. Despite appearances, the difference between these would-be friends and the Labatut caravan poses a significant question, as important as the distinction between vertebrates and invertebrates, between governors and the governed, between believers and nonbelievers.

Thinking about the Labatut caravan, the thought crossed my mind to set up another ledger, which might clarify my position on language—that is, the balance sheet of the net profits realized by corporations and individuals on the work of Arthur Rimbaud since his death. Here's my estimate, with a margin of error of plus or minus 10 percent:

1. Successive editions in 43 languages — 10.1 million
2. Public and private sales of manuscripts and original editions — 3.5 million

3. Publication of critical and biographical essays by researchers who owe their careers, whether in France or abroad, solely to the accumulation of Rimbaud factoids (minus the cost of theses, travel, and secretarial help) — 40.5 million

4. Radio, TV, and movie adaptations dedicated to the life and works of the same author — 54.5 million

5. The traffic in booklore realized on the products mentioned in categories 1 and 3 — 4.2 million

6. Photos, posters, badges, medallions, and handbills — 1.0 million

Total: 113.8 million

Something on the order of the annual salary of a senior executive at the Google Alphabet Holding Company. So you've turned a profit on young Rimbaud's death. But has it really paid off big? Nothing, compared to the new social media and financial sectors.

That's why Yves Bonnefoy is right to see in the above-quoted Rimbaud poem entitled "Sale" (from *Illuminations*) a cynical commercial metaphor signifying "the corruption of the initial aspirations of the poet into shabby, finite and inert objects." He's absolutely right, provided you include the royalties collected by Yves Bonnefoy in the total 113.8 million of the Rimbaud enterprise account, not to mention the one-thirteenth of royalties that some courageous publisher will have to refund me for publishing this book. (Since Rimbaud isn't cited in the other chapters, I'll keep this pittance for myself.)

In a very different world, I would be happy to see an end to the posthumous sale of sacred and profane relics, and to the neglect of the precious remains, in favor of the often trivial but deeply stirring forms of life—such as an actual face, an actual encounter, or a true handshake.

If it takes too long for that to happen, I'd

rather breathe my last than witness the throng
of flunkies jostling one another on the slopes of
profane Golgothas, fighting over the corpses of
people they wouldn't really want to associate with
anyway—phony admirers of the dead.

But as for death itself, so sweet, so calm, so
eternally betrothed, why avoid it? I certainly
wouldn't.

It doesn't matter much to me whether the poet
(Rimbaud himself) swallowed or spit out the
holy wafer during his last rites. Instead, I'd rather
find out for what amazing reason nobody has said
anything about his *words*, the dying last words
of the Living Man, whispered into a confessor's
ear. Is it out of respect for a secret considered
untouchable? That would surprise me on the part
of those who are partial to silence and lacunae.
Or is it, rather, because of the belief, academic
and hagiographic in nature, that nothing remains
of great men except their written traces? In any
case, nobody has bothered to find out what the
much-vaunted *troubled priest* actually heard from
the mouth of Rimbaud.

In this significant oversight I sense the visceral fear of imagining, through others' examples, the frightening spectacle of one's own death rattle and, at the same time, the embarrassed indifference—mingled with a genuine pity—that one is supposed to feel for that deplorable state: the unhealthy delirium of any ordinary dying soul or the discreet disgust that one also feels for any stricken brain, now rendered commonplace by so much suffering.

Finally, if the Rimbaud cultists had taken seriously their own lyrical flights with regard to the *Illuminations*, they would have shown more interest in his last words, fallen upon the ears of a priest.

❖

I'm afraid the moment has come to describe another experiment. The method, the procedures that I'm here deploying might seem, at first, to resemble those of the hagiographers whose ill-fated effects I have just criticized, but what I have found, what I am in a position to offer, cannot be enclosed within the circle of chance or power.

37

Arthur Rimbaud entered the Hôpital de la Conception in Marseille on May 20, 1891. He informed his mother and his sister of this in a telegram dated the next morning, which spoke of the extreme gravity of his condition:

> *Monday morning, amputation of my leg. Near death.*

> *In a word, our life is an unending misery! So why do we exist?* (Letter written to his sister Isabelle, June 23)

> *I shall go to my grave, while you shall walk in the sun.* (Isabelle's notes, Sunday, October 4)

Next, the business with the chaplains—the last communion and confession. I paused over this passage of Isabelle's letter to her mother, dated Wednesday, October 28, 1891:

> *He's saying strange things, very softly, in a voice that would cast a spell over me if it weren't so heartrending. What*

*he's saying are dreams—yet it's not
at all the same as when he's delirious
with fever.* **It's almost as though, and
I really believe this, he's doing it on
purpose.** [My emphasis.]

*As he was murmuring these things, the
nun said to me in a low voice: "So he's
lost consciousness again?" But he heard
everything and he blushed deeply; he
didn't say anything more, but, once
she was gone, he said this to me: "They
think I'm crazy. Do you agree?"—"No,
I don't think so. . . ."*

You can't accuse Isabelle Rimbaud of inventing
myths at this particular conjuncture. Still reel-
ing under the effects of her emotions, she hadn't
distanced herself sufficiently to begin elaborating
the posthumous legend of her brother. On the
other hand, it's possible to compare the preceding letter to her recent reading of the *Illuminations,* whose "supernatural visions" she evoked
in a letter sent on October 12 to Paterne Berrichon. As for visions, the very last message from

39

the poet—in a letter that he dictated to Isabelle on November 9 to the director of Messageries Maritimes (a shipping company)—resembles the invoice of the Labatut caravan more than it does the *Illuminations*:

> *one lot: a single tusk*
> *one lot: two tusks*
> *one lot: three tusks*
> *one lot: four tusks*
> *one lot: two tusks.*

> *Tell me when I'm to be carried on board.*

All this is well known, all this has been glossed by voluminous scholarly commentary, but nobody has looked into the confession itself. In the letter to her mother of Wednesday, October 28, 1891, Isabelle wrote:

> *When the priest left, he said to me, looking at me with a strange, troubled look, "Your brother has faith, my child, what in the world were you telling me!*

*He has faith, and what's more, I've
never seen such faith."*

A December 30 letter to Paterne Berrichon
speaks of two confessions. The Rimbaud zealots
have run on endlessly about faith—which wasn't
the real issue. That question's only real purport
was to shore up two legendary sagas: the religious
one, fostered by Paul Claudel, and the profane
one, fostered by the Surrealists. Both sides based
their interpretation on the Seer, the Alchemy of
the Word. If the worshippers had for one moment
believed in the power of words in any sense other
than posthumously, they would have pondered
the effects of Rimbaud's final confession.

In early December, I went to Marseille to visit
the official archives in order to consult the reg-
isters of the former Hôpital de la Conception.
During one brief hour of research, I found the
names of the chaplains assigned to ministering
to the patients during the fall and winter of 1892.
There were three of them: Abbés Claude Girard,
Louis Servin, and Anselme Coulemas of the sec-
ular order in the Marseille diocese.

In the archives of the diocese, I found no trace of Abbé Coulemas. I saw that Abbé Servin had remained assigned to the Hôpital de la Conception until his death, in 1912. As for Abbé Girard, his case merits full attention: the pastoral register mentions his withdrawal from the hospital in December 1891 for a "nervous ailment" and his being sent to the psychiatric hospital of Saint-Ylie, in Dôle, in the Jura region, where he had relatives.

At Saint-Ylie, in the medical archives, I found the following among the notes of a certain Dr. Kruger (folder E.H. 12 through 22):

> —*January 17, 1892. First interview with Girard, abbé of the Marseille diocese. Obsessional mania, not dangerous. The patient eats, sleeps, and moves about normally, but cannot engage in any coherent conversation. To questions relative to his past life he invariably responds, "Allah Kerim! Allah Kerim!" and then begins to sing aloud. So far as we know, he has not served in our African missions. Has he*

*spent time in Muslim countries? We
don't know. Cold showers and sleep
will help him recover his memory.
Fluorine hydrosulphate. Herbal teas
as a palliative and sleeping pills.*

*—February 22. Nurses report that
Girard speaks oddly but on a variety
of subjects. Progress. However, the
other inmates of Pavilion B group
themselves around him to listen, even
at mealtimes. Report these groups to
me and take notes on the patient's dis-
jointed remarks.*

*—March 19. Girard seems to have
recovered his faculties. But this
improvement is accompanied by
a curious identity crisis: thus, the
patient claims his first name is Arthur
and not Claude. He speaks of travels
in Europe, to Java, to Cypress, then
to the Middle East, to the Somali des-
ert, to Harar, Aden, etc. He especially
mentions another country that nobody*

here ever heard of: Aséré or Aseroé, it
remains unclear.

—April 21. Isolate Girard for one or
two weeks. His strong influence on the
patients has led to a kind of collective
delirium. Fear of violent attacks. The
nurses aren't watchful enough. What
are they afraid of?

—May 20. This Abbé Girard is strange.
He asked to see me without waiting for
the usual appointment. When we were
alone in my office, he took hold of my
head very gently and told me unbeliev-
able things. I've never heard anything
so beautiful. I am troubled.

—May 22, 1892. Yes, at last, WE ARE
IN THE LAND OF ASÉROÉ. I am
Dr. Kruger, but is this really certain?
I . . .

Here the medical record breaks off. The regis-
ters contain nothing else relating to Abbé Girard

or to his doctor. I did not find the name of Girard on the release records, although I pored over them from 1897 to 1940.

I decline to pursue the inquiry concerning Dr. Kruger. Let others, more qualified than I, carry on. . . . As for the land of Aseroë, I know, alas, what to think of that.

3

Aseroë

THAT INERT OBJECT, bespattered with black markings and which represents the written page, offers no organic life, no soul distinct from its flesh. In that restricted space where the eye momentarily encounters it, it barely manages to conceal those memories or expectations that it transforms into costume jewelry or a child's chipped cat's-eye marble, bird feathers, yellowed photos, or a gold chain. But supposing that the reader's vision emerged altered by the work? Would light and shadow no longer clash? Rimbaud's *Noël sur la terre*. Christmas on Earth. The rediscovered baubles of childhood, the awkwardness of angels entangled in their own splendor. And as the light of day breaks, colors seem

invented, today, for the first time.
(6:12 A.M.)

On February 12, rereading these lines scribbled in a notebook three days earlier—from "that inert object" to "colors seem invented, today, for the first time"—I traveled to the city of Semur-en-Auxois to haunt a house lent by a friend.

At lunchtime, I went into the Café du Donjon and sat down far enough away from the bar not to be disturbed. The waitress spread out paper place settings, set white dishes on the tables, decanters, bread, and wineglasses. She bustled about cheerfully, her bright virgin's face dappled with sherbet and kisses.

There were a few patrons, mostly oldsters. A woman entered holding the hand of a tubby little girl whose stare alighted on me and never strayed till the end of the meal. When the waitress announced the menu (fresh vegetable appetizers, andouillettes, boiled potatoes, a tray of cheeses, coffee—all for fifty francs), the girl giggled agreeably. Her mother showed her to a table and sat next to her. With an easy, tender motion innocent of any impatience, she wiped the girl's childish chin, tied the napkin around her neck, and ran her hand over the child's hair.

Sitting at my table, three times I crossed out and recopied the sentence running from "That inert object" to "colors seem invented." Bright sunlight was streaming into the room, despite the thick frost on the windowpanes. As a child, when I was ill, I would sometimes experience this same high degree of light and would anticipate its caress approaching my face and enveloping me. On this particular day, I was not feverish; my mind, alert to the point of cynicism, declined the surrender I might have otherwise welcomed. Let me hit them with a line of poetry, I thought—a nasty impulse immediately shunted aside by the sensation of completely blanking out, of feeling completely drenched in light.

Objects became sharply outlined; bodies were rendered readable: veins on the skin, strands of hair, wrinkles and crow's-feet on the face, the fibers of the clothes. Each voice, despite the slight humming in my ears, called out to be heard, to be acknowledged. I crumpled the pages of my notebook (where I had written of "baubles," of "angels" and of "colors"). Instead, I watched and listened.

The air was stirring around us; I was aware of its currents, its sworls; but what magic was suffusing this café that smelled of *frites* and tobacco? "Eat!" said the mother. The girl moved her head and waved her right hand above her plate without lifting her eyes from me. "Look at your plate, and eat!" I lowered my eyes to escape her too-insistent stare. I became awkward. My glass of red wine, overturned on the tablecloth, stained my abandoned pages, but this accident did nothing to break the charm: the sunlit dirty walls, the smirched tablecloths, the dumb smiles, the smell of fried fat.

The girl's stare bore down on me again. Her right hand dropped the fork and moved back and forth in the air, her thumb glued to the tip of her middle finger. Confronted with this obscene gesture, I lowered my eyes and then saw, under the table where she was sitting, her fat legs, her cotton stockings, her snow boots. She was pissing with joy! One of her legs was drenched, while she continued to wave her wrist over the table. The mother grabbed her daughter's hand and put the fork back in it. "Eat, Nathalie."

Everything was covered in white light. The bread, the cheese: heavenly manna, its taste heightened by the brightness. Sadness, disgust were gone. Everyone was feeling what I felt; I could tell by watching the surprised faces of the guests. Some were lifting their hands to touch the air; some were laughing like children.

The needles of ice on the windowpanes—melted by sweetness?—parted to let the bright rays shine through, forming stained-glass windows of mother-of-pearl, opened like wings. The fake flowers on the bar counter became as white feathers, beaded with blood.

The idiot girl started to stir again, looking for my glance, waving her obscene hand. A cruel thought assailed me, and I made an effort not to shout aloud "Let her sing, the little fool! Let her sing once or twice in her life, the little bitch!" What she sang wasn't exactly Orpheus's song, as you might well imagine.

Mouille mouille paradis
La femme est à l'abri
Mouille mouille paradis
Les agneaux sont guéris.

Paradise, cream in your jeans
A woman by any other means
Paradise, cream in your jeans
The lambs are full of beans.

The little idiot was onto me. Crazed with delight, she dropped her piece of cake, hid her face in her mother's bosom, and then grabbed at the waitress's apron in passing, demanding her pencil and order pad in a whiny voice: "Lalie wants to draw! . . . Gimmee!" " Shut up," said her mother. "I'm going to take her outside; she's too worked up." The waitress said, "Wait!" and looked behind the counter for another pad, another pencil. "Here, Nathalie, you can write and draw all you want." The mother agreed, all smiles.

The light was a pearly white, coating every object in its caress. I considered this carefully, holding my breath so as not to break this gathering force by a single word—just as a single first step might crush the eggs of insect larvae barely hatched between the soil and the dew.

Now the light was chasing away all the shadows with frightening speed. The frost tightened its grip on the windows and, for a fraction of a second, the rays, diffracted by the crystals, traced an orange star upon the tablecloth where Nathalie was seated.

The girl was waving pages scribbled with circles, crosses, and hatchings every which way. "All done! All done!"

Gone was the charm and play of light. The bistro returned to being a mere bistro: cheap drinks, coffee, grease, and smoke. The faces were extinguished. "Leave it there. Come, come on! . . ." The mother got up and took her daughter by the hand.

Nathalie stuffed the papers into one of her pockets; her mother dragged her to the door. But as she was about to leave, the little idiot wheeled around and marched up proudly to me and placed the papers on my table.

I looked at the torn pages she had offered to me. Circles, crosses, hatchings (the uncanny parody of some unknown form of handwriting?), but also featuring real letters like *S,A,E,R,N,O,G* ... Then, on another sheet, these three lines, carefully scripted:

A*É*O*É
L'ANGE É PARTIE
J'É LU DANS TES PENSÉES

A*E*O*E
THE ANGEL WEN TAWAY
I RED YOUR THOTS

4

Aseroë

I HAVE NOT BEEN SPARED from the ravages of forgetting. I wouldn't be able to point to the exact street or to the house in front of which all this took place.

First, there was the *Concert of Angels* on the Isenheim Altarpiece, their fiery garments the same hue as those November vineyards back then in Colmar, and the Virgin with her incandescent crown, of which I had had a premonition the previous day, gazing at the starry sparkles of the local Moselle wine at the bottom of my glass. . . . But, most of all, there was the presence of Gunther and Claudine, whose friendship shielded me from difficult days.

I'm often haunted by those who've died young. Today I'm again haunted as I think of Claudine, my act of writing transforming my uneasiness into a species of terror, once I come to realize that all those who have died before their time, all those who never even had the chance to reach their prime, have now suddenly become my *elders*. Their faces have thereby achieved the status of icons, their smiles hanging frozen in the air, not as they might appear in past snapshots, but now frozen in the very air before me, at moments when I was sure they had completely vanished from my mind.

I find the streets and houses of this town quite uncanny, bearing as they do the imprint of some-one now gone. Were I to return here, all these fine façades would be wrecked for me, as would the cathedral. The rain would be unremitting; everything would turn ugly before my eyes.

I hear Claudine laughing and making her little sarcastic comments, which so manage to impress and seduce both of us. I'm not talking about her beauty here, but about her voice, about her quirks of thought. We are carried away by her gaiety, but as soon as she has managed to draw the two of us into her mirth by a well-placed quip or caustic observation, she waits for just the right moment to deflate our laughter, brutally reminding us what fools we have been to fall for her dumb little jokes. Then, having reduced us to utter embarrassment by some dry or cutting remark, she then starts up again, captivating our bemused attention by commenting on this or that passing face or scene that she has just noticed as we three make our way down the street. In short, she loves leading us along by our noses. Which is, of course, why, without letting her know, we so adore her.

I had more or less forgotten all about her when, three years later, I received a long letter from her containing poems that struck me as rather arty. After signing off with "xxx kisses," she added the following sentence, which I also thought was just a young girl's daydreaming: "When it comes time to get out of here, we'll take everything along with us, the entire world, meaning even Gunther, and even you."

I wrote her back a letter that received no reply; a month later, Gunther wrote to tell me that Claudine was dead.

The *Concert of Angels* and the lovely face of the Virgin have retreated behind another more ancient altarpiece that I glimpse upon entering the Unterlinden Museum in Colmar: its Paradise, Purgatory, and Hell are just as terrifying.

Claudine is walking ahead of us, pointing to the panel of infernal torments to show us the figure of a woman utterly racked with pain. "You'll soon get a good look at her," she said. "What do you mean, *soon*?" "You'll soon see her, if I manage to find her, and if she agrees." These unsettling words erase the boundary between this picture of Hell and our present life. I shrug my shoulders, suggesting that Claudine just take in the painting in silence.

Several hours later, after we have all had lunch, we cross a public garden and then wend our way through one narrow street after another. Standing in front of a stoop is a tall woman— very dignified, very erect. Every now and then she raises her hand to greet someone we do not see. Claudine leans into me to say, "Here she is, the woman in the altarpiece." I recognize the pallor of her face, creased by deep wrinkles. In fact, she is looking at nobody; her eyes are cast toward some unknown place beyond the neighboring houses. She is waiting. Her right hand, slightly outstretched, bears wounds above the palm. Her other hand is clenched against her belly. . . . We pass by. The woman raises her hand to her mouth and bites at the wound, then extends her hand again without appearing to suffer; then she curls her lips into a grimace, and then brings her hand back to its earlier position.

I turn to look at her and observe the same cruel gesture repeat itself, slowly, obsessively: hand moving to mouth, mouth biting at the wound, grimace, relaxation of hand, hand again outstretched, then reaching toward mouth, mouth biting hand, mouth grimacing, then relaxation of hand.

I observe her wound—violet, swollen—which returns again and again to welcome her bite in a very precise cadence. Not a single complaint on her part, not a single murmur.

Claudine explains in a completely matter-of-fact fashion: the Occupation, her husband tortured to death by the SS under the eyes of his young wife and in this very house, below the front stoop, which she now refuses to leave. She goes to do her shopping; she chats with her neighbors. There are days when they see her prostrate in front of her door. They say of these days: *her hand is going nuts.*

I no longer hear Claudine's words. My mind, my body are beyond sick, shot through by commands sharper than arrows: *"Auf die Knie! Hände hoch, Jude!"* "On your knees! Hands up, Jew!" My stomach is turning; I feel my head emptying out. Little by little, a memory that is not mine erases my own recollection. I no longer have the energy to fight back against this mental intrusion. Why should I be forced to relive something I myself never experienced? Horrible thoughts assail me on all sides. I hear blows addressed to me from the past. I undergo these blows. The SS breaking into the house, then the fake search of the premises carried out by the underling thugs, who toss around the furniture and destroy whatever lies within their reach. I feel the kicks addressed to my belly and to my face. They strap me down on the kitchen table so I might witness him getting his teeth bashed in and his fingernails ripped out. Why? Because he is simply guilty of existing, guilty of having a name. Four men hold him down on the tile floor; a fifth man pummels his face into a bloody mess and pisses on him while barking orders. The man is already dead, but they keep going after him. "Get him to talk!" They keep on beating him; they want to leave him more than dead. Their hatred knows no end.

I have no more *I* at my command to write to the end of this scene. As I extend it and retract it in order to gnaw at it, can my writing hand attain any sort of definitive solution that might at last release it from these irrevocable deeds? I bear witness—but without having witnessed anything of the above. Time is out of joint, projecting me toward a past that is not mine. The disaster is so intense, it echoes far ahead into the future.

This grisly state of possession gets all mixed up with a memory that is far more mundane: the memory of a documentary that included German newsreels from the year 1939. It's springtime, and the *Mädchen* are dancing in the fields. There they are in a circle, cavorting around the Ideal Aryan Girl (the film is in black and white). The Ideal Blonde is clutching a bouquet of daisies, her fair locks are wafting in the wind, and she is puffing light tufts of dandelion into the breeze. I see their seeds disappear into the sky, a lie on the level of SS spittle. I hear the Nazis chanting their anthems. Flags, the whole military-industrial complex, people in uniform, goose steps, *Heil Hitler* salutes. The images all blur: the young girl's lovely hand, her fresh breath, the flowers, the shouts suspended in air, the tortured hand of a madwoman who reminds us of everything we forget. The two figures—the picture of youth subjected to propaganda and the picture of youth subjected to torture—are overlaid. I am driven by a dark instinct to disentangle these two scenes in my mind's eye. I am driven to submit to this command: "Remember that which you have never experienced!" But this hand *going nuts* is something that cannot be forgotten. The permanence of the wound cannot be stanched. It is the Devil bowing and bussing your hand.

Placed as she is on her stoop, a statue made of flesh, this Altarpiece Woman does not see me. A Cassandra of modernity at its most abject, is she enough to conjure away this massive act of forgetting—of which she knows absolutely nothing? Is she enough to stave off that most sickening expression of such forgetfulness—namely, "communication"?

Mouths functioning without words, and words without mouths, each disarticulated from the other. That lips should move, speaking in order to say nothing, that lips should impose onto other mouths the oblivion of speech, that words in exile should collapse into one another or throw around their weight on various wavelengths, intercut with the hurrahs of sports fans or canned laughter—all this astonishes me, all this fills me with dread.

I would like to reread these pages and substitute the words with others. I do not recognize them; they no longer belong to us. I can hear the command: "On your knees! Hands up, Jew!" But I can also hear the lines of one of my favorite German poems: *"Händen des Mädchen von einst und jetzt"* ("The hands of this girl of now and yore"). There is no throb of the heart strong enough to cancel—be it by a succinct universal phrase—the infinite distance that separates the person who tries to speak, and then to sing, and the person who pays no attention to his mouth, spitting out crazed discourses of extermination.

❊

The birth of a word, and then of another, invented by woman. The day when the wound will be healed. Which could be a secret, or the avowal of a secret: to stop "communicating," lest you become monsters—that is, empty "whos" and empty "whats" subject to the empty questions tossed back and forth by the Major Powers of Communication. To learn to speak—simply— as before . . . With the murmurings of small children in tow. And with the sheer song of vowels or consonants also providing an escape from the embrace of the void.

5

Aseroë

M<small>Y</small> F<small>EBRUARY</small> <small>VISIT</small> to the Accademia in Venice, the emotion felt facing Giorgione's *The Tempest*—the flash of lightning suddenly seized—and my reading one year later, in a catalog of the Château de Tanlay, of a letter written to Giorgione by his poet friend Antonio Brocardo. I wrote a short story in which I identified myself with the latter, claiming that from 1480 to 1510 I had worked in Giovanni Bellini's studio as well as in that of Giorgio Barbarelli, who was known as Giorgione. Thus, I would have been a rare witness to this *capture of a flash of lightning*.

In this short story (later abandoned), I shrank away from my own private sensory impressions—under the pretext of fictionally embodying an earlier existence I had never experienced—but why did I refuse to open my eyes? Apart from the historical meaning of *The Tempest* or the disturbance provoked by my observation of this work, the reading of a letter of which I believed myself to be the author had encouraged me to maintain that this ancient canvas contained AT THE PRESENT TIME *a visible thought*. A thought, translated by artistic means, but in such a way as to move it forward in time—as if just short of or just beyond the possibilities of figurative representation.

I would have granted that Giorgione might have wanted to destroy his painting, having despaired of providing a representation of the impossible; and also that the magic of the lightning flash, according to the aesthetic of the end of the Quattrocento, might come down to us several centuries later as somewhat dimmed or unpersuasive. And that the capturing of the lightning flash would remain what it has never ceased to be for art: an impossibility comparable to the lack of lived life in even the most vibrant of Early Renaissance portraits.

I recall my feelings at that time. It was midwinter and I was looking at the painting and, without making the slightest movement, was anticipating an event, although I didn't know of what sort. Soon, I sensed that a light was flooding the space and illuminating the soldier and the half-naked Gypsy woman suckling her baby. I was caught up in the landscape of the painting. The lightning flash removed the shadows and traversed the objects without reducing their opacity; it enclosed and traversed me, as well.

I've seen hundreds of visitors pass in front *The Tempest*. Some would only react after having identified its signature (ah, Giorgione's *Tempest*!); others would pass by without noticing anything whatsoever. My behavior was unusual enough to trouble me for a long time after my visits. At the end of prolonged contemplation, the lightning—fictionally restrained within the limits of the frame—agreed to offer me the blinding explosion I was anticipating. The original strike of lightning was, as it were, restored by a second flash, in which time was deferred and perturbed by a double emergency—the initial jolt of the painter who had managed to fix this flash in an immobile duration, and its subsequent seizure by my admiring glance, which had to follow a reverse path, resolving the lightning's original duration into an abrupt effulgence in the now. I suspected Giorgione of having foreseen such a result, but how and why?

I remember several stormy nights in mid-August in the Ardèche. I saw the clouds crumble down and burst over the Meyrand pass and the lightning illuminating mountain and valley. But the fascination exerted by Giorgione's work doesn't stem from some sort of painterly, representational "truth"—even if the painter's art stirs in us the most vivid impression of a resemblance to what nature displays to us in the blink of an eye. In *The Tempest*, the most ephemeral moment of suddenness and the most prolonged moment of duration both undergo a violent reversal that modifies our fundamental perception of time.

It's possible that some obscure motivation leads me to exaggerate. Is Giorgione's procedure as singular as I had thought? Any portrait requires this same finesse: a smile, a subtle gesture, the intent of a gaze are as difficult to represent as the sudden flash of a storm. This very rational train of thought led me to abandon the above-mentioned short story, which would have necessarily led to my utter confusion.

But seven months later, I was somehow again caught up by my own story. I found myself at that time in a state of mind in which the mere mention of Giorgione's name or that of any artist would have made me laugh self-consciously.

On the evening of September 22, contrary to my usual habits, I ate and drank more than was good for me, and went to bed quite out of sorts. Very early the next morning, I left home and wandered on foot through the forests as far as Châtillon-sur-Seine (a hike I undertake once a year). A remote inn on the banks of the Ource, near Voulaines-les-Templiers, was my intended goal after the first leg.

I was walking at a steady pace, admiring the sky, the impressive plant life, and all the things that came into my view at every turn of the road: the sod huts of the old foresters, the bushes with their nesting birds, the carpets of

77

moss smirched with bloodred *muscaria* mushrooms, the animals here and there.

Late the following afternoon, I sighted a
grove of elms among the oaks, these tower-
ing trees, spared from the disease that had
ravaged their species, formed a perfect circle.
Their majestic crowns commanded the respect
of all the other nearby forms of vegetation. In
the middle of this circle, the low grass lay like a
freshly mown lawn, presenting me with several
clusters of wild orchids—the delicate *Ophrys
apifera,* or bee orchid.

Seated between two elms, I observed the col-
umns of light between the branches. Evening
was falling and the sky was smudged with clouds.
Suddenly, several gusts of wind altered the lie of
the clouds and the storm broke, rapid and bot-
tomless, with unexpected intensity. I stood
there, soaked from head to toe. Just preceding
this uproar, a vivid flash had lit up the forest. It
died out almost immediately in the approaching
half-light. One or two hundred yards behind me,
lightning fell upon the clearing. A shredded elm

pointed its blackened splinters toward the sky. I ran off, gasping for breath, and without looking back, headed for my inn.

The next morning, still frightened by the intensity of the storm, I gave up on pushing toward Châtillon-sur-Seine and returned to my home in Plombières as soon as possible. During the miserable night spent in the inn, I had discovered that *The Tempest* and Antonio Brocardo's letter to Giorgione (which I had read for the first time two years earlier) were fragments of one and the same work, a diptych simultaneous in its optical and mental image—the painting and the epistle indissolubly comingled into a ✷ choreography of time.

I needed to verify this. Since I couldn't return to Venice, I gathered together some reproductions and I read and reread Brocardo's letter to his painter friend. Surprise and alarm amplified my initial enthusiasm: to capture the lightning as Giogione had done would involve far more than creating the mere illusion of freezing time. I sensed that the painter had engaged in a mercilessly lucid act—to gamble his entire project, as well as all his artistic ambitions, on a fraction of a second, on the sudden disappearance of himself. One can read the watermark pressed below the surface of the sky of *The Tempest*: "Everything is about to disappear. Everything shall disappear."

This visual thought—neither a lament for years gone by nor a mortification intended to instruct us to forget the vanities of this world—has no other purpose than to exalt the ephemeral, to praise the stubborn persistence of movement, to extol the precise stroke: the passionate leap of the dancer ahead of a fall.

This discovery modified all my convictions. It gave new meaning and an entirely different cast to certain facts—later associated with Lausanne and Budapest—whose true import had until then escaped me.

At the moment I'm writing this (fall equinox, 6:34 A.M.), I have before my eyes the following sentence of Robert Walser's, written toward the end of his life: "Write while dancing." And also these words that Suzanne Cordelier attributed to an exceptional dancer (La Argentina) on May 10, 1936. As legend has it, she addressed a full house, overwhelmed with emotion: "I'm quite willing to dance some more for you, whatever you like, but I've run out of music." Followed by renewed applause as the curtain came down and the lights dimmed and the dustcovers were draped over the velvet of the loges. The image of La Argentina entering her house two months later and collapsing on the threshold. I also have before me a little photo of Vera Ouckama Knoop, the sight of whom inspired Rilke to make a last effort at writing his *Sonnets to Orpheus* and his final *Elegies*. Images lost in infinity, in the depths of a hall of mirrors, drowned in the All that is Absence. Farewell, face (captured in a snapshot). Farewell, dance figure. Farewell, final whirl of death.

A poem, a painter's glance: the finale of a requiem for fleeting beauty, a requiem for disappearance.

I can easily imagine the conversation encouraged by true friendship: Giorgione said to

81

Brocardo that in a dream he had seen Apelles' fresco in the temple of Artemis at Ephesus, *Alexander and Lightning*. The sky on fire—unrepresentable—was pictured this single time. But of this ancient destroyed temple we have no trace—nor any evidence of Apelles' painting. The lightning, reclaiming its divine rights, must have erased the profane image. I imagine this dialogue and I think that Giorgione must have bettered Apelles by far, having represented both the flash of lightning and the disappearance of the mortal who had witnessed the flash.

Now (April 16, 6:45 A.M.), I'm looking through a magnifying glass at an excellent reproduction of *The Tempest*. The colorless light has no source. Despite the painting's patina of age, I perceive a bolt of lightning composed of every hue, including black. On either side of the river, the young man and the woman and child are calm, far too calm. Are they awaiting the promise of another life? A glow envelops them all, as well as the walls and the foliage. Night and day escape from the controversy of contrasts, gathered together in the heavenly storm.

82

I think of Giorgio Barbelli—that is, Giorgione—as a brother. The black death snatched him away. His days were numbered. His poet friend Brocardo, who fled Venice because of the war, sent him letters that went missing. In the years 1480–1510, the French king's League laid waste to the villages of the Veneto and the plague broke out amid the devastations of war. On May 13, 1510, Giorgione received a final letter from his friend Antonio Brocardo. Here it is, translated from Italian:

> *Dear Giorgio, How pleasant it is to stroll the city streets, as the peripatetic philosophers and the wise men of old once did, speaking of our cats and of the hidden face of the world. By respecting my silence you have strengthened my taste for reticence. Sans image, what good are words? Mere pebbles rolling along a riverbed where we two cannot walk abreast, forced to proceed with our noses to our feet, without seeing anything of the world, without anything possessing the slightest*

meaning—except that we're moving
forward like beasts. I can see very well
where we're headed: we're about ready
to believe in the power of speech, to be
caught up in its game. What a wonder
the power of speech, yet how harsh and
pure its exile, which so cuts us off from
life. Speech is within us, yet we're also
caught up inside it. Once the ink of
words is dried on paper, there's nothing left around us but immense solitude—or death upon the shores of the
sea. All is nothingness. But among the
ashes of words I know very well that
we would continue to write to each
other, like children, with our fingers.
I can clearly see what it is that obliges
the two of us to write or paint: it's that
naïve desire to bring time to a halt, to
take up residence in our solitude once
again. We want to go on living via our
signs, having now become the gods of
our own immortality. But what a useless thing to pursue: this cult of immortality. If we cannot know how to live,

let us at least learn to die. Our work is like the faith of the simpleminded. The sound of verse is its surest music. We are attached to signs that create a chain, binding man to man. And yet, it is only from the depths of our silence that we speak; it is only as solitaries that we come together as men. But are we yet sufficiently alone to be free? Life is such a small thing that one could easily withdraw into one's room in order to invent the world. Again and again we repeat the same signs with new images. Come on, my special friend, we so enjoy living that we shall find pleasure in it in the end: let's rediscover the delights of writing and of painting in quiet rooms. Our ultimate vanity. As if the only legitimate love were the love of absence. They say the plague is now general: take good care of yourself! Otherwise I would never have been able to speak to you as I have.

6

Aseroë

A FTER A WEEK'S WORK in Budapest in November, I decided to spend my Sunday at the National Museum. The next morning, in Szentendre, on the Danube, I was to meet the painter Endre Bálint; he was going to show me the façades of the old houses featuring the "Serbian motifs" of which I was ignorant while looking at his drawings several days earlier.

The trip to the museum was painful. I was asleep on my feet. The paintings were running in a blur before me; I had to make an effort to distinguish one from another. My week's work, which was quite interesting and proceeding at a regular pace, didn't explain my fatigue. I was afraid I might be falling ill, but I had no shivers, no discomfort—just a strong urge to sleep. All these rows of paintings seemed unbearable to me: bloodless nudes, idiotic portraits, nauseating crucifixions, ponderous battles. The visitors seemed to be accomplices in all this. How could I put up with their murmurs, their admiring commentaries? I was afraid some annoying person might notice my deplorable condition and denounce me as a spy. I immediately made up my mind: I would walk through the galleries at a swift clip.

I was moving along quickly from gallery to gallery, going against the direction of the tour. I raced through several centuries—the Italian Primitives, Spain, Flanders, the Renaissance, and the Baroque—a few seconds for each period and country, nothing more.

Since the rooms were well heated, I began to feel reinvigorated. Several times I passed in front of the same canvases. "No point in lingering," I told myself toward the end of the morning tour, impatiently waiting to be hungry enough to make my exit with a good excuse.

❧

A little later, I was stopped dead in my tracks in front of *Caterina Cornaro,* by Gentile Bellini. "Stopped dead in my tracks" is the right expression to describe my condition—for almost the last two hours, any sense of "culture" had been lost on me. Seized by sudden delight, I spontaneously discovered a face—with whose eyes, whose hair, and whose Venetian coif I fell instantly in love.

Talented, elegant, and flattering as the painter's treatment may have been, it wasn't the beauty of the face that captivated me but the sparkle of her look, the intense emotion that animated her. Resisting too hasty an infatuation, I took the time to examine all the details. I observed her forehead, her mouth; I roved lovingly over her hair, her eyes, her cheeks. It was as if her material surface were troubled by the loving caress of my gaze. This idea seemed to please the painting, and its face smiled back at me. I immediately assumed that I was the victim of some visual disorder or the effects of a fatigue too recent to be entirely overcome. I wanted to clarify the situation, and, holding my breath, I approached the portrait. The actual canvas of the painting, now so close to my eyes, became even more disturbing. Who was I to accuse, down to the last detail, the clumsiness of Gentile Bellini, who had left all the vestiges of his numerous pentimenti so poorly covered up? Had the artist interrupted his progress at several points of his painting, leaving it at the sketch stage, neglecting numerous delicate nuances, botching the finished work? Or rather, did every flutter of his brushstroke anticipate that fashionably *négligé* manner that would later become so common in the art of the portrait?

I feared the worst: despairing of finding the overall truth of a face, had the painter simply attacked its individual features, drowning his finest touches under a poor glaze, thickening the color where he should have instead lightened it? No, the portrait was irreproachable: you just fell in love with it the moment you saw it.

The painted surface came to life before me. It made me think of those faces that sleep with their eyes open: they're motionless, but you have no doubt that they're alive. These sleeping beauties never gaze at their onlookers, but this Venetian woman by Bellini was staring at me intently. One would have to find the source of movement, however slight, that justified this illusion. The painting was immobile, and my glance was not distracted. I imagined that there must have been some phenomenon in the air—between my face and this painted face—some change in the atmosphere, some alteration of the light, to which I had failed to pay sufficient attention.

I moved this way and that in front of *Caterina Cornaro*. I observed the other canvases as well (with their perfectly inert faces, their formal beauties), but again and again I returned to *Caterina Cornaro*. The flesh coloring of her face remained ever vivid—a striking anomaly that at once called out to me and made me afraid. Meanwhile, I vehemently rejected any notion that I was here encountering a real woman in the flesh: I preferred the sensible inertia of an image completely divorced from its deceased model, the expected absence of a being whom I would never come to know. In an ancient portrait such as this—quite the reverse of an image glimpsed in a mirror—is not the evocation of a woman supposed to be an image frozen in time?

I leaned forward once more. My gaze sought out the eyes in the painting and met them, lost in anticipation—a summons that refused to die out. "Your painted face clouds over the moment I look at you, yet your eyes are begging for life." These were words I whispered to the painting, but what did they mean? There was a subtle exchange between us. "Your gaze is insisting on the life it lacks." I concluded: Yes, it's as if she were begging me, and I closed my eyes, utterly in love.

❧

Deprived of a model for several centuries, the figure in the painting was crying out for a live woman. The relationship between face and portrait had in this case been reversed. Time itself, like some inept god, had been annulled. "Caterina!" she was saying, "Let your face come forth; let it agree to correspond to mine feature by feature!" A crazy request, which I was at a loss to answer, but which I sensed as I stood before her. I addressed the portrait in person. A voice rang out in the silence of the gallery, filled with joy and anguish. It was not my own.

Later, I turned around. The visitors were passing by *Caterina Cornaro*. Nobody was looking in my direction. They didn't know that a painting was in the process of awakening, engaged in a freakish argument with time. The ancient gaze was calling out to me. But it was not entirely aimed at me. Instead, it stared right through me and sought out a woman—the model who was yet to come and who would at last appease the portrait by finally offering up its lost resemblance to it.

Feeling like a rejected lover, my eyes left her face to wander over the patrician interior of the museum, inspecting its furnishings, its wall hangings, its dimmed bedrooms—the prison space that kept the deceased Caterina from stepping out of her frame and rejoining me in the here and now.

Then I turned away from her portrait. On the wall facing it were windows opening onto a lighted space. I made my way out onto the cold street, just barely tinged by the November air, and headed for Kálvin Tér.

Unable to focus my attention, I walked around for a long time. The painted face wouldn't leave me alone. I tried to act decisively, but went on one fool's errand after another. At one point, I bought some Serbian and Bulgarian periodicals, although I didn't know a word of either language. In another place, I bought a pocket mirror I would never use. Several times I took the same bus in both directions—the number nine, from Kálvin Tér to Déak Tér, from Déak Tér to Kálvin Tér. I was humiliated by the painting; I needed to find a life that was less haunted, a life made up of ordinary things. Finally I got back to my hotel and went to bed without dinner, exhausted by my errancy and the endless stream of cars.

The next morning, I was glad to meet up with the painter Bálint in Szentendre. We walked slowly through the alleyways; he showed me the designs on the windows, the wrought-iron decorations, the statuettes, pointing out the various architectural details of the houses. The old man often halted in the middle of his sentences to catch his breath. We drank some coffee as we spoke of painting; then he left, making me promise to come see him before I left Budapest. I was planning on buying two of his drawings. They are in my study as I write this: a tumbril for the dead, the seventh arcanum joined to the thirteenth, both the color of dawn—black, blue, white.

One hour later, I settled into a *börözo* (a cellar tavern) and ordered some excellent *kéknyelü* from Badacsony, some bread, and some fruit. I had brought along a book of short stories by Kostolány and picked out a quiet spot in a corner.

I found the reading so riveting that I lost track of time, and when I looked up it was getting dark. The *börözo* was filled with customers who had just finished their workday. Glancing behind me, I saw a group of young people and two lovers who were kissing passionately. A drowsy old man was trying in vain to raise his head, and next to him, on the other side of a pillar, a young woman was writing letters. She had seen me arrive, had smiled at me, and had forgotten me the whole time I was reading (though I was watching her, distractedly, while appearing absorbed in my

book). When I finally closed the book, I studied
her features, her fine, long hands, and, as I looked
at her pointedly, trying to remember where I had
previously met her, she got up, arranged her letters in a blue canvas bag, approached my table,
and introduced herself in German: *"Ich bin die
Katalin Koszorú. Hallo, François."*

I invited the young woman to sit down, looking for a way to let her know—without appearing ridiculous—that I had already made her
acquaintance. She picked up my book and leafed
through it, putting on a serious air, as if to make
fun of me.

"François, I saw you at the National Museum
yesterday morning. You were standing in front
of Gentile Bellini's *Catarina Cornaro,* and I
was behind you, against the window that you
noticed just as you were leaving. Take a good
look at me, I'm asking you."

I complied with her request somewhat reti-
cently, for I knew I would have to admit that I
was here faced with a striking resemblance to
the woman in the portrait. I was thinking about
leaving as soon as possible, I was looking for any

98

pretext, but Katalin interrupted me, placed her hands on mine, and said with a smile, "Relax, I'm just going to sit here and read."

❧

She opened the book, more or less in the middle, and told me how I had spent the previous day, dredging up the most minute details I had remembered. Alarmed, I heard her pronounce, word for word, the very sentences I would have formulated had I been asked to describe my disarray in front of Bellini's portrait. I protested halfheartedly.

"You made it up. That's not in the book, believe me."

"Come on, you know very well I'm not joking." She took up Kostolány's book again and began to read from the same tale—the tale of how I had spent yesterday.

"Katalin, the tale you're telling me isn't in that book."

"On a certain level, I understand you, François. What I'm saying isn't in any book. All the same, here, just take a look. . . ."

With her finger, she showed me page seventy-eight, where I read "All these rows of paintings are unbearable for me: bloodless nudes, idiotic portraits, nauseating crucifixions, ponderous battles. . . ." I paled. Katalin leaned over and kissed me.

"So, do you recognize me now?" She drew nearer, placed her mouth to my ear, and murmured: "Katalin, Caterina, Katalin, Caterina . . ." She laughed at my confusion, then began to speak very rapidly about her work, about her hobbies, about her life. Her family lived in Pécs; she had two brothers and two sisters; she was taking business classes, but she really liked painting and cinema. When speaking of her everyday life, she made use of the words "my daily routine"—*mein Alltagsleben* in German—which hardly reassured me.

A few minutes later, she took my hand and placed it on her belly. "I'm expecting a baby; you can feel him, can't you?" I touched her belly. My hand shook. "Yes, yes, I can feel him." I ran over in my mind the first name of the woman whose belly I was now touching: Catherine, Katharina, Katalin, Caterina. "Come to my house," she said.

100

❖

We left the cellar and walked in the dark, without uttering a word. In front of her house, Katalin looked for her keys under the flagstone at the doorstep, opened the door, and pushed me ahead of her. "Go upstairs, François. I'll follow."

In the bedroom, Katalin proudly raised her dress up to her breasts, and in a low voice uttered this command: "Kiss my belly, François, and take me slowly, very slowly."

At the back of the bedroom, on a dimly lit wall, hung the effigy of *Caterina Cornaro*. Her glance was calm now, but the image was empty. The woman who was offering herself to me had gently assumed the ardor of that ancient face.

❖

I withdrew from Katalin; then she said in a hoarse voice, "Kiss the little one, François, kiss him with all your heart, or he'll die."

Aseroë

I placed my mouth between her legs, and there I spoke, there I sang. It wasn't in the tongue of Goethe or of Bembo, but in a tongue—Katalina's—whose meaning escaped me:

> *Fölfedett engem balra–jobbra*
> *leomló társak kártya–szobra*
> *elém tárul a tér ragyok*
> *min úgyse változtathatok*

"That's enough! Now get up and leave, François! You must forget me forever."

7

Aseroë

THERE ARE PROCESSIONS of words; beneath every funereal word the dead are gathered, beseeching us to lend them the power of saying "I" one last time. Is this voice our own?

The words travel from mouth to mouth, from book to book; a murmur arises and grows progressively louder as it disappears. Over the course of this process, stories fall to pieces; others, patched together, arise to replace them. Tawdry metaphors abound; in order to come up with a single decent image, the spoken word lacks a true road on which to travel from its origin to its final destination. I know nothing about this road; in the end, I allow myself to be led along by a language I do not know. Though I don't really understand it, at times it seems to offer itself to me without my noticing.

The Testament of Orpheus, germinal words, a guardian angel, an aphasic Cassandra, a witness to lightning, the portrait of a young woman at once innocent and perverse—all these figures of forgetting guide my sentences. The procession of words goes from oblivion to oblivion. Each word, a sign of death and of life, of defeat and annunciation, relates the return of Orpheus, but his full story—barely glimpsed—escapes. I may collapse before finding what needed to be said in order to secure solace. Orpheus does not exist—which is why he so disturbs us.

Orpheus, precisely. I traveled to Laon with B. in the early fall to see a fourth-century mosaic on which an anonymous artist had represented the god, his lyre, and the beasts charmed by his song. The forms seemed naïve, but I liked the composition and the palette of colors—blues, greens, golds, blacks.

For the unknown author of this work, the Orphic songs were already nothing more than simple nursery rhymes, but they still preserved the glamor of magical formulas. A few centuries earlier, Apollonius of Rhodes—at the beginning of his *Argonautica*—attributed this double mission to Orpheus:

> *. . . To say what I had never before*
> *set forth . . .*

> *. . . To insist above all on the dire*
> *necessity of the Chaos of yore . . .*

What can song still mean when the memory of a disaster as old as the world is mingled with the urge for an originating word? Those who wish to listen are few in number. The shops, the churches, the streets, the loudspeakers all speak at every moment of the death of Orpheus—hands clapping at the announcement that "The Price Is Right," tinny slogans, canned laughter. I no longer hear common nouns. Have meanings been stripped from every verb, have names been removed from every object? So many real yet invisible wounds. Zombie words wandering here and there, looking in vain for their correspondence to things.

In the thickness of lies, oblivion precedes every memorable deed; poems are nothing more than thin fissures—cracks that refuse a world where the violation of light and song announces nothing but atrocities to come. On the road to Laon, I heard shouts in broad daylight. I was overcome with anguish. Cries calling out, me unable to answer.

❧

The Laon mosaic occupied a wall in the great hall of the municipal building. We asked for a key from the concierge, who told us, "Except for a few foreign tourists, I don't get many visitors. It's a room where children go to draw." On the other walls, we saw gouaches and collages, with bright colors, guarded by a row of antique busts—Cicero, Demosthenes, Caesar—which hadn't been used as models for decades.

Before leaving the room, I saw a dog at Orpheus's feet. This unobtrusive dog had neither the grace nor the radiant colors of the wild beasts and birds summoned by the master of song. The dog was listening without drawing attention to himself. I should have noticed him sooner, for this animal belongs, like the lyre and the Phrygian cap, among the attributes of Orpheus. What sort of role could such a dog play in the legend? Was he capable of following his master into Hell and returning unharmed? The ancient poems say nothing about this; but the moment I saw the mutt, so modest, so attentive, I ceased to imagine the celestial transports caused by some primordial sound- and light- show (Chaos, Night, Day, the original Logos . . .) and I said to myself, My place is among the eternity of beasts! We humans are now lower than the animals. Dumbed down by our modern surroundings, we no longer understand a single thing. I should be like this dog; that would be ideal! To become as Orpheus' dog—this, luckily, still remains a possibility. Rilke, my most constant companion, would not greet the idea with sarcasm. In his Eighth Elegy, the song rises to its apogee the moment he recognizes in animals the VISION OF THE OPEN:

What IS outside we know solely by
the face of the animal; as for children,
already too early on, we turn them
backwards and force them to see, from
behind, readymade forms, and not
what is open, which, in the faces of ani-
mals, is so profound, so free from death.

Yes, act like a dog, before writing a single line of verse. Several weeks later, in Montpellier, at a time when I had an appointment with "Captain Hatteras," I was dragging around my carcass here and there. I felt too low to appear in public, and at one point I started following a mongrel dog, a cross between a pointer and a terrier, who had obviously lost its master. I followed it step by step through the Peyrou garden, down the length of its beautiful alleyways, around the trees at its corners, and wound up in front of a balustrade, where the dog agreed to nuzzle up to me. From there I observed the Roman aqueduct, which extended beyond the central lane all the way, so I imagined, toward Saint-Guilhem-le-Désert.

Instead of keeping me company, the dog abandoned me. Bereft of my new companion, I followed a winding path through the narrow streets of the city, which took me all the way to the Place de la Comédie and rue de la Loge. It's silly, but I was depressed because of a book. I needed to trace out this particular route because I was stuck on one of its pages, endlessly bogged down in an Orphic proclamation whose enigma continued to resist me:

> THOU SHALT FIND A SPRING TO THE LEFT AND A WHITE CYPRESS. TAKE CARE NOT TO APPROACH THIS SPRING. THOU SHALT FIND ANOTHER FROM WHENCE FLOW THE COOL WATERS OF THE LAKE OF MEMORY. BEFORE IT STAND THE GUARDIANS. AND THOU SHALT SAY UNTO THEM . . .

I had sworn to fill in the ellipses of this final mutilated command (from a golden plaque on a sixth-century BC tomb), but I despaired of ever succeeding.

The probable conclusion of the fragment must be a password—the formula without which Orpheus would never have succeeded at his task. "I AM A CHILD OF THE EARTH / AND OF THE STARRY SKIES." I admired this sentence, but my familiarity with it did little to diminish my anxiety. Its words had lost any clear meaning: the way they were used in ancient Greek signifies that we (as humans) belong both to this Earth and to the far-reaching heavens, that we are the children of an Earth rendered fertile by the light, but the Greek words that once meant Earth, Sky, Light possessed spiritual overtones that have long been lost.

Today, numerous barriers block out the echoes of even the simplest song. How was I to restore the ancient text? By skipping over the time-out demanded by Buchenwald and Dachau? By delivering myself of the occasional poem that attempted to bemoan this disaster? By executing a sheer leap of the soul?

I wept as I walked, keenly aware of the ridiculous dead end I had reached in my attempt to
decode *The Testament* of Orpheus. I was thinking of an idiotic dream I had had several days
earlier: The Poets' Society had summoned me;
the event was taking place in a shabby room
(an attic room?), a cramped room bursting at
the seams, with distinguished poets squeezed
together, each one remaining, in spite of the
presence of the press, aloof from all the others. Some of them were declaiming while
pretending not to, others were weeping, still
others were snoring, but upon my arrival there
was an outburst of sarcasm: "The cur! The cur!
How wretched he looks with his short hair!"
I wasn't proud; I was gripping in my pocket a
very wrinkled piece of paper onto which, that
very morning on the train, I had scribbled this
quotation from Virginia Woolf, lifted from
one of her journals: "Art is inadmissible. Yet
the absence of art would mean that society as
a whole had turned into a nightmare without
end—the boundlessness of thought upended
into the boundlessness of horror."

At that point, a dismaying idea occurred to me—of the sort that always causes me to rise up in revolt. Instead of wasting your time mucking around in some ancient text, why not spend your time on worthwhile and socially beneficial causes? You're getting all stirred up over nothing; you'd be better off spending your energies on taking some sort of immediate action against everything it is you loathe. That's when I felt like hitting somebody. I needed a scapegoat to justify the miserable fact that I had decided to give up writing, Any journalist or pollster or top-notch executive would do. It could be just about anybody: the arbitrariness of my action would be matched by arbitrariness of their misdeeds— just as long as I had the opportunity of slugging someone for no reason whatsoever. No, that was too cowardly; what I needed was a *real* victim, a completely innocent bystander.

I espied an old man, oddly dressed, hunched over, carting around his shopping basket. He was shuffling along quite quickly on his bandy legs. Just a flick of a finger would be enough to topple him over. Then I would courteously come to his aid and pick him up again, casting the blame for my assault on some imaginary passerby. Here was a real challenge, worthy of our times. After which, I would do away with myself—assured of not suffering any consequences.

I was about to proceed as planned but was held back by a ludicrous detail: my intended victim was talking to himself aloud as he shuffled along. I caught up with the poor wretch; when I held out my arm to touch his shoulder, he turned around as if he had sensed me coming all the while and shouted out at the top of his lungs:

"She told me so."

❖

The old man kept heading toward the market. I followed him as far as the wholesalers' stalls; a woman, all smiles, hurried toward him to put some vegetables in his basket. The old man just stood there shuffling, without turning his head or uttering a word of thanks. He frowned, all the while casting his eyes down at the ground and up to the sky. Then he was off again. At a butcher's stall, he shouted the same sentence out aloud—*"SHEETOLDMEESOO"*—and again farther along—*"SHEETOLDMEESOO"*—clearly enunciated, with the same vehemence.

The man moved on at a steady pace, his basket now filled, his shoulders sagging. As he moved along, his feet dragging in their oversize slippers, every twenty or thirty yards he would repeat the same refrain—*"SHEETOLDMEESOO."* The passersby watched and grinned. A girl pointed him out to her mother: "Look, Ma, it's the prophet!" Other people turned around, shot him a glance, and just shrugged. A shopkeeper said to her daughter, "Go give something to the loony!" Again the old man stopped, shuffled in place, frowned, and looked at the ground and into the distance. Then he was off again, shouting out:

"SHEETOLDMEESOO . . ."

An idiotic refrain: the reprise of an unknown disaster, the echo of a broken promise, of a grief too grievous to be shared? A caesura? You have

catastrophe

116

nowhere to go and yet here you are shouting, claiming that a woman had said something to you, but what? Admit it, forget it, fill the gap with a random tic, a random gesture, a cry in the night—and transform it into this pathetic, magnificent outburst addressed to nobody in particular in broad daylight. Some children were laughing. I couldn't blame them. Their easy laughter and his wounded words were two parts of the same poem.

It's hard to kill yourself, and it's almost impossible to do so when the time is no longer right. You let yourself be carried along by the painful slippage of days, your memory in disarray—the loss of a wife, the absence of a lover, the disappearance of friends. You get up, you go to bed, you get up again, you put one foot after the other. The litany of pain.

The old man was leaning against a wall, having put his basket down. I approached him and whispered into his ear, *"Aseroë."* Without so much as looking at me, he replied, "Exactly!" He picked up his basket and went on his way.

117

Farther on, before crossing the street, he again shouted out, *"SHEETOLDMEESOO."* Then he shuffled past a school and disappeared, still in search of some ancient promise, now cruelly consigned to oblivion.

8

Aseroë

It was in April that I met the Japanese choreographer Hideyuki Yano for the first time. I had admired his *At the Hawk's Well*, inspired by Yeats. Yano had succeeded in seamlessly blending the mythologies of Japan, Africa, and Europe. This had enchanted me. I loved the balletic duet, *River Sumida Madness*, that he had composed with the African dancer Elsa Wolliaston.

Yano had come to Dijon for a dance workshop and that spring, engaged as I was in editing a certain book, I found myself at a very low ebb, unable to establish the most simple relationships between words and feelings. I sensed that my language was betraying me. The very act of writing seemed like some nasty ordeal I had to undergo before gaining access to a single clear thought. I had just devoted several days and several nights to the perception of blackness, engaged in what

I called my *séances noires.* Since the eyes tend to become accustomed to darkness, gradually adjusting to all the tiny gleamings it contains, I had prepared several darkrooms, which I had carefully sealed against any intrusions of light. I needed to mislead my sight, to remove it from any known object, to devote it strictly to the apprehension of absolute blackness.

By keeping my eyes open as long as possible, by not allowing my vision to seize on any single point of reference, by losing all notion of time and space in a completely darkened room, I thought that these "black sessions" might allow me to discover thought in its purest—and most perceptible—form. I had no delusions: I didn't expect to achieve absolute lucidity at the end of each of these voluntary seclusions. To achieve a healthy state of stupefaction would be sufficient. I was fully ready to embrace idiocy, provided it might help me to discover an unknown connection between writing and feeling. I hoped that out of these séances of darkness, words would emerge—vivid words, innocent of any lie, words devoted to the simplest of perceptions, virgin words.

At several points, I tried my hand at writing in total darkness, hoping to seize the moment—which would then immediately disappear, like dreams at the moment of waking. Each time, I had to overcome my body's stubborn resistance. In the end, I had to recognize that I had failed; in fact, I had even (predictably) regressed, tormented by the amnesia and the anxiety traditionally referred to as *la petite mort*.

Far from having diminished the separation between perception and writing, I had only increased it. But the fact that I had failed only reinforced my absurd conviction that it was my duty to persevere, to proceed onward without any determined goal in mind. I would solicit the powers of innocence at some other time, and in a different fashion. The pitiful result of this series of self-mortifications was a manuscript about fifty pages in length, which I was cruel enough to submit to several friends. I knew I was putting them in an awkward position: they were, after all, aware that I wasn't doing very well and therefore wouldn't dare tell me how they really felt, afraid as they were of hurting my feelings.

When Yano came to Dijon that April, a month had passed since I had finished writing up the sessions of my *séances noires* and I was ready to forget those pages. However, after lunch, Yano asked me what I was writing, and since he had just mentioned that in his work as a dancer he had always wanted to prolong words into the silence of gestures—to invent, as it were, a *danceword*—I described to him—without concealing my difficulties nor my ultimate embarrassment—the paltry little adventure to which I had sacrificed so much time. As I was describing my obstinate path to failure, I saw that he was raptly listening. In my retelling of my adventure, a drama was clearly taking shape in his mind—one in which I played no part. I fell silent. The silence lasted a long time; then I heard him softly pronounce the following sentence, as though he were protecting an invalid:

"Night is indeed our house, but not one I could ever enter while talking."

Yano begged me to lend him my text and advised me to read two works by the Japanese novelist Kōbō Abe: *The Woman of the Dunes* and *The Wall*. A few months later, I met J.-M. in Paris; he asked me if I would agree to allow Yano to use my *Séances noires* for a dance piece. I asked J.-M. to convey my sincerest regrets. I wanted nothing more to do with this text.

I saw Yano again in Besançon in December, for the second and last time. He was presenting a piece produced by his dance workshop. At the end of the performance, we spoke briefly. He interrupted himself in the midst of a conversation having to do with contemporary dance, and turned toward me. The sentence he spoke hovered between an affirmation and a question.

"What beauty in the art of falling."

I learned of Yano's death through friends two years later. It was only then that I opened *The Woman of the Dunes* and *The Wall*. At the end of the first short story in *The Wall*, this passage seemed addressed to me:

*How was it possible that there was a
blank everywhere my name should
have been signed? Or was it that there
were only things that refused to call
out my name, or else refused to have it
mentioned?*

Further on, another sentence alarmed me, for
I thought I was hearing the voice of the deceased
dancer, at a slight remove:

*Yes, I do indeed possess a house, but
where at the moment find the "I"
capable of entering it?*

How to sleep after that? But the night was
not alarming: I saw names, processions of
names, parading along like living beings. Some
of the names were speaking themselves out
loud; others were joined together into a cas-
cade of phrases. The names were peaceful, at
once light and self-assured. It was enough for
me to hear these names to feel absolutely happy.
The absence of this dancer, who was almost a

stranger and who had understood me so well, was shining like a star.⏐

Among the names, I hear HANA—Crystal Flower of the Dance.

I also hear AS **T** AR **T** E, goddess of air and of water, white and black, fecund-fecundating.

ASARÉ, ÉVOHÉ

ASÉROÉ, ÉVAHÉ

CHOROS, CHARA

To impart at least a bit of meaning to this madness: The road of excess leads to the palace of wisdom. The dance is not finished; the thread drawn by the Fates cannot be broken. It weaves the invisible fabric of language, its scattered consonants and vowels intertwined, then snipped apart again, then reknotted. Yano-Hana-Crystal Flower has left his gestures, his words behind. To others, he lends the names he no longer owns.

❁

Night—a thickness, an excess, a vanishing of light. For those who look at night and utter

its name aloud, the obscurity that ensues constitutes a kind of monstrous OUTSIDE, without entry. But obscurity—at least the vision one
gains of it on a clear night at the end of July—
can provoke a troubling sensation. A night that
bathes you in its absent rays.

In the night, all possible space gathers into
itself, and dissolves. The void suddenly calls out
to you, freighted with meaning. Behold me here,
absorbed into the very thing that had eluded my
grasp. In order to look upon the night, I need
to forget its name—and this forgeting becomes
the extreme form of memory, the very vigil of
its origin.

9

Aseroë

IT WAS SPRINGTIME in Lausanne and I was looking for a book. I was offered the opportunity of consulting it on the condition that I wouldn't name its owner, who was worried about greedy book dealers or crazed collectors. The book lay before me in the half-light, shielded from the jealous illumination of an overhead lamp. It was the original edition of *La Cena de le Ceneri* (*The Ash Wednesday Supper*), published in London by Giordano Bruno in 1584. I'm not speaking of the octavo edition—the only one mentioned by bibliographers—but of the unique quarto edition, cited by the Polish mathematician Jósef-Maria Wronski in a letter to the banker Arson.

My host removed the book from its blue casing, put it down before me, caressing its vellum binding (which was without any ornament or title). Slowly, he turned the flyleaf and read aloud its full title, emphasizing each word: *The Ash Wednesday Supper, Described in Five Dialogues by Four Interlocutors, with Three Reflections on Two Subjects.*

I first had to listen to the story behind this unique book, written down by my host on a strip of grimy cardboard. Before being arrested by the Inquisition and burned alive in Rome on the Campo dei Fiori, Bruno had offered this book to Gaspar Schoppe. Later, this unique text came into the possession of the astronomer Kepler, then made its way to the Vatican Library, from which it was stolen in 1722. It resurfaced around 1800 in a shop in the Hague, which belonged to a bookseller named Jakopus Krüger. According to a chronicler of the Court of Nassau, this bookseller lost his sight from having pored over Bruno's black plates at too great length, hoping to discover in them the traces of a celestial body that the author had neglected to indicate. In 1813, Wronski saw this same work at a bookseller's in Berlin and praised its "unheard-of splendor, which approaches the Absolute of Numbers."

If an alert hand had not saved it, this precious book might well have disappeared at the end of the last century in the fire that consumed the Altenburg Castle. The man who showed it to me that April claimed he had received it from an Italian collector who had, in turn, procured it in London from the Indian mathematician Srinivasa Ramanujan, who was as much a devotee of esotericism as he was of algebra. My host had saved a strange letter of Ramanujan's, slipped into the pages of the book, which he translated for me. In it he discussed "the dance of numbers whose enigmas, always followed by temporary solutions, in turn engender new enigmas and further solutions—each one disappearing into the other without entirely erasing them, each one observing a whirling, spiraling movement comparable to the escape of the Universe beyond the limits that the mind assigns to it. . . ." It was at this point that I heard the following sentence which my host was kind enough to copy down for me: "The darkness of night is the index of an infinity that never ceases to expand and whose color is that of a future without origin."

I let my eyes rest on the eight black plates of *The Ash Wednesday Supper.* The engraver, no doubt guided by Giordano Bruno himself, therein represents night by broad, flattened surfaces on which the pattern of the stars and the geometrical tracing of their relative distances stand out in white on a black background. The plates of the unique Lausanne edition—in contrast to those of the octavo edition (which I later consulted in the library of Chantilly)—are printed across the entire page, with no margins. The black is so dense and so velvety that I thought I was seeing—thanks to an ingenious trompe l'oeil effect—the actual night sky in the book. Its blackness might have been obtained by soot, but I doubted that a printer could have fixed soot in his ink without staining the other pages. I thought of the *heliogravure* prints of the end of the nineteenth century, which impart a matte quality to the tones—a depth that subsequent photography hasn't been able to duplicate. "Burnt bone and horse-hoof glue! Burnt bone and horse-hoof glue!" exclaimed my host with a satisfied air. I shuddered as I thought of the sad end of Bruno, roasted alive for a book—this one, precisely.

I was asked to leaf through all the pages, without skipping a single one. I admired the typography of the text, each chapter head individually composed for each Dialogue—and of course the black plates. I stopped at the last page, which was immaculate. "Keep turning, keep going to the very end!" On the verso of the last page, my friend pointed out a form that was scarcely visible, a tiny figure of Vanity embossed into the white tissue of the page: a crowned skull, and these mottoes, which I read at an angle beneath the dim beam of the lamp:

MORS SCEPTRA LIGONIBUS AEQUAT

❖

OMNE SUBLIME VIDET

Giordano Bruno was clearly connecting Death (which "levels kingdoms," posing the funereal violence of the spade against the pride of scepters) and the eminent Eye, which sees "all high things." The second phrase, borrowed from the Bible (Job 41:34) primarily designates the invisible gaze of the Most High, but in another (and far more disturbing) reading, DEATH becomes the subject of the infinitive TO SEE. If Death allows access to the sight of the Sublime, or indeed if Death itself *constitutes* this sovereign gaze, the final motto (almost lost in the fibrous white of the page) suggests to the attentive reader a meditation on the Hidden Book of Averroës.

My host affirmed that Bruno, motivated by his quest for the alchemical Great Work (for which the scepter and the holly are the emblems, as well), wanted to place the reader on the path toward the Great Secret. . . . This made me quite uneasy, for it seemed I suddenly was losing my ability to read and that the embossed mottoes themselves were staring at me, drawing me toward the abyss.

When I was about to close the book, my host placed his hand on mine. "François, you haven't finished reading." He gently withdrew from the vellum volume a sheet the size of a quarter of a page, a black plate even more admirable than the others. I noticed that its delicate white lettering was arranged like the stars of Sagittarius: NOX NOS INTUERIT—*night observes us.*

❖

Rue Lucinge. That April night in Lausanne pursued me beyond my actual encounter with the book, or indeed with the plates with no margins whose black fiber opened out onto the very night sky itself. I searched out the starred letters, which might reveal Bruno's secret to me. A disturbing sentence came to me: "Death's gaze is swifter than Light." If someone had such a gaze at his disposal, wouldn't he therefore have sped back to the beginning of Time? After which, deprived of Light, wouldn't he be then returned to the Night from whence he had emerged? He wouldn't exist, or at least not yet. . . .

$$\sqrt{\overline{\frac{\varepsilon}{8\pi\,b(\mathfrak{t})\,\supset}}} = \frac{I}{H(\mathfrak{t})} \equiv T\exp(\mathfrak{t})$$

Each time we are presented with someone whom we can love, it seems to me that the raptness of our attention snatches her away from her mortality: we are seeing her for the first time, her face smothered in kisses. Isn't this what the onset of Time really involves? There in Lausanne, on rue Lucinge, I dismissed all these worrisome thoughts. The darkened windows, the frigid houses, the Swiss tameness of the place all struck me as fake. I had found myself there by mistake, pursuing a false illusion. But then I saw a woman passing by. She turned to me and smiled.

❧

I remember she was very beautiful. Within myself I was singing: Let's follow this angel, let's finish the night.

What does the woman Lena have to do with this story? Is she here to disprove me? To cast a spell on some obscure book? To give way to dawn? On rue Lucinge, smiling and weeping at the same time, Lena led me to her home. Once there, she had me go upstairs, to no purpose. I spoke to her of Bruno and of the *Ash Wednesday Supper.* "The poor man," she said, oblivious to his fiery end. She told me the sad, uneventful story of her life. I listened to her as she spoke and whimpered like a child. As I got up, she asked me, "So do you want to?" "No," I said, "it's not worth our while." "Too bad," she replied. As I left her home, she uttered the following sentence, which might have been prompted by her state of fatigue or intoxication: "Night is the graveyard of names."

Two days later in a Lausanne bookstore, I came across a volume devoted to the Orphics. I read the following words, which are rather different from those of Hesiod, which I have never forgotten:

> Black-winged Night was seduced by the Wind and in the Darkness she produced a silver egg. From this egg sprang Eros—whom some call Phanes—who set the Universe in motion.

10

Aseroë

THERE WAS THIS MAN—the simple truth of the matter is that I was in his way and he wished me no harm. I had bumped into him, and he swore at me and shoved me against the wall of the Jardin de l'Arquebuse in Dijon. That's the way it was; I would have done the same if he had been the one blocking my way. He shouldn't have stared at me. *Stared at me* is perhaps too strong a phrase, since he was looking at the wall. As far as he was concerned, I didn't exist. The look he cast at me was without any concern or disdain for me; it was simply indifferent, and for the first time in my life I found this intolerable. In fact, it felt like torture. It's not that I'm over-sensitive: had he thrown himself in my arms, I would not have tolerated it; even too insistent a look on his part would have annoyed me. But I felt my privacy had been violated by the very mindlessness of his gaze.

A frank indifference seems to me the best

policy when encountering a passerby, but something had changed on that December evening. It had nothing to do with either of us; it was a product of the changing times, of which I was only dimly aware. A major event had taken place without my so much as noticing it—unless the nature of this event was such that the horror of its occurrence had insidiously disappeared, once one's attention had been diverted from it.

I've sometimes run into a friend after a long absence and not recognized him. The passage of time tends to erase people's earlier features, but this is not what frightens me. What I am attempting to describe is perhaps so heinous and so harmful that I would be better off not mentioning it at all. The delivery of certain looks and certain words that involves intricate acts that are sucked up by the cold or buried by the grave. Are such acts a way of carrying death within oneself, before it actually arrives? Are they based on ignorance of the fact that death will occur come what may and in its own good time? What does it mean "to carry death within oneself"? Have all distinctions collapsed? Do death and life no longer differ? Have they become interchangeable?

❊

That December evening, near the Jardin de l'Arquebuse, the following sentence had taken shape in my head. I repeated it over and over without understanding it: it was neither a proverb nor a sudden insight, nor was it one of those arresting thoughts that come to mind while one is just strolling around:

> *Many are those who give life without*　❦
> *an ounce of tenderness.*

And then nothing more. I was talking to myself. I saw a man running and he shoved me against the wall, swearing aloud. I wouldn't mention this insignificant fact if the man hadn't turned, if I hadn't noticed his face near mine, if I hadn't immediately feared that the worst was being called down upon me. Death is less frightening than the ill will of some ordinary man, but here I was finding myself face-to-face—in the course of a single interminable moment—not with death or with a random stranger, but with a creature who struck me as absolutely inhuman.

Why this sudden aversion? His manner, his features seemed amiable enough, and on some other occasion I might have found this passerby pleasant enough. His face was almost handsome, and seemed unmarked by any trace of suffering or illness. I like most faces, as long as they are not looking at me askance. I have, of course, had occasion to encounter faces burned out by lies or by the lust for power; and I have met with other faces corrupted by hatred. But this was not the face presented by this stranger. He cast me a look that was foreign to this world. In fact, he cast me the absence of any look— and it is the memory of this that turns my blood cold. And yet this look seemed almost familiar to me. It was as if over a period of many years I had become inured to this level of horror.

It was difficult to admit, but I had just bumped into someone utterly repulsive, a creature lacking any humanity. This idea disturbs me, for when I was young I used to clip newspaper photos of murderers, of torturers, or of notorious tyrants, which I then mixed with photos of scholars and artists. I noticed then that, when taken out of context, the names attached to these various faces could be interchanged without their features thereby needing to be modified. Having just written that this man was "a creature lacking any humanity," let me admit that I am sure of nothing of the sort. He could have just as well been an angel as a devil.

It is both the fear of the unknown and the sway of common prejudices that causes us to abandon our curiosity and to see only grimacing ghosts instead of human beings possessed of no other magic than their strange appearance. Would this account for our hallucinated visions of the war-painted faces of rival tribes, of the maws of carnivores, or of the plague-stricken unfortunates who wander from one town to the next with their walking sticks, their bells, and their masks of crows? Organic transformations can prove to be just as fearsome: serpents sloughing off their skins, the mating rituals of insects, or scenes of birth whenever witnessed at close hand—the infant with his eyes glued shut, his hair stuck to his deformed forehead, his mouth contorted and then shrieking out at life, more grotesque than a death mask.

The bestiaries of old and the chronicles of

the first explorers communicate to us the panic experienced when one is confronted by some unknown species. Pliny the Elder says that the *catoblepas*, located at the sources of the Nile, is a midsize beast whose gait is lazy and whose head is so heavy that it cannot carry it on high—the head simply droops earthward and drags in the sand. The author adds that this particular infirmity is a boon for humans; otherwise, they would succumb to its murderous gaze. It's possible Pliny was libeling a mere South African gnu, but what am I doing with my poor stranger? Am I treating him like another *catoblepas*? Or like some humanoid or mutant? How does the repulsion he inspires in me differ from the most common garden variety of xenophobia?

Over the course of my life, I have seen faces ravaged by fire, others by the butterfly rash of lupus. I shall never forget the pocked faces of the lepers I saw in northern Bamako, near the river Niger. I wouldn't use the word *repulsive* to describe a single one of them. If my stranger were to cross my path again, I would not dub him "a creature lacking any humanity." This spiteful observation, which haunted me that December evening and in the months that followed, now makes me feel ashamed. Because I know that this face could have been my own.

During the whole day that followed this encounter, I was ill, incapable of doing anything. My passionate negation of a person about whom I knew absolutely nothing caused me to throw my own well-being into question. By trying to cast this encounter into words, by trying to somehow name it, wasn't I getting off on the wrong track? I'm not saying this out of any pretense toward artistic sensibility: I mean what I say. I am overwhelmed when I think of the final madness of Friedrich Nietzsche. I can see him throwing himself in tears upon the neck of that beaten horse in Turin. I hear these words; they stagger me:

> *Parched*
> *By the truth,*
> *Do you still remember,*
> *Do you still remember,*
> *O burning heart,*
> *The thirst you felt back then?*

❀

That December evening, I sensed that the train of thought that had been opened by the *Anthurus archeri*—that is, by the "devil's fingers" in the form of *Aseroë*—needed to be brought to a close or else to change in such a way that the words at my disposal—designating not only a very ancient form of life but also an originary lightning strike—would have to undergo a violent crisis. This time, I feared I was confronting a trial beyond my capacities. The frank indifference of the stranger, which was equal to my indifference to the hurrying crowd, did not lie at the source of my disarray. I know that our laziness causes us to simplify the faces we see. Wasn't it I who, jostled by a passing stranger, neglected to register the details of an ordinary face, reducing it to a few summary odious features that served my purpose? I was imparting a false appearance to it—a convenient mask of Otherness.

❧

The late afternoon of July 21 (my birthday) found me sprawled out on an armchair in front of the television. There was a very cheerful master of ceremonies hosting a strange game: the television audience, men and women alike, had been invited to create on live TV the stylized portrait of their ideal man and woman. While the women described over the telephone (you could hear their live voices) the features of their dream man, a computer recorded their votes as to some detail or another, and from this collection of desires the machine averaged out the features, which were then gradually projected onto a giant screen. The technique of the "robot portrait" (or "Identi-Kit"), invented by the police to profile potential suspects, here found its televised application. In my mind, I saw the rather handsome creature who was being here suggested: he could have been a reporter or a young CEO or the master of ceremonies himself—who did not fail to point out, in jest, his close resemblance to the media meme of the ideal man that had just been computer-generated.

Suddenly, as the eyes were finally being drawn in on the computerized portrait, I saw my passerby of December emerge from the intense light. His inhuman face, his stylized features were henceforth more than probable. I imagined the proliferation of these clones. Statistical indifference having become the norm, there was only one step left to be taken in these times of crisis and generalized panic. Only racist violence could resolve this nightmare into broad daylight. Any statistical deviation from the norm, as slight as it might be, becomes a handicap for the victim. This process of "othering" is propagated slowly and insidiously—every day a little more—and generates its own crop of wops, coons, wogs, or gooks in every city, in every district, in every family. The desire to eradicate the half-breed, the métis, to eliminate the Other from the circle of the living—an absurd but entirely realizable proposition—will express itself more distinctly over the media. How modern: to smile at the very strangers you want to eliminate.

I looked at myself in the mirror. I've been affected; my appearance has changed. Words, having lost their individuality, fail to express my disarray. I thought enviously of that Australian tribe that created a new word each time one of its members disappeared. Whereas with us, language under the impress of the various media undergoes an opposite fate: at each birth, another sentence disappears. Language will disappear by attrition. Already, during the night, personal pronouns suffer from anemia: the penury of nouns and verbs forces them to slash each other to ribbons. Every morning, in front of the mirror, the faces tormented by this nightly combat remake a mask for themselves. It's vitally important to remove, as much as humanly possible, any personal emotion. Gone are distant gazes, the tentative inquiries. Competitions, stereotypes, knee-jerk reactions, sound bites, blogs, tweets, tabloids, sports, video games, and, from time to time—like the attacks of malaria every four days—hooligans from rival soccer teams going at one another, or attacks against immigrants. CAUTION: KEEP YOUR DISTANCE.

The nameless arcanum is not attached to the number it announces. Unbeknownst to me, it lurks within the twelve chapters of this book. Coming from without, where books are humiliated by being deliberately ignored, it already stalks a child I once loved and indirectly attacks what I hold most dear. This morning, July 21, I'm waiting for the boy in the yellow sweater, holding a bouquet of daffodils in honor of my birthday.

11

Aseroë

IF, UNBEKNOWNST TO ME, any attentive reader were to venture to gaze intently at the white page I wish to offer, if any reader were to make an effort to probe its apparent emptiness with all the passion required by an undertaking on which this reader's life would suddenly depend, would I at last be satisfied? If my project—come to maturity some time ago—at last found its completion in the adherence of this ideal reader, then a path leading to the Other Language might finally open, a path paved with desire and longing, capable of carrying both of us into the land of the marvelous, into a never-ending story.

For some time, I have been envisaging some space to come that would be devoid of all inscription, a space where only the gaze of the other would manage to embody my thoughts, where the precise meaning of everything I had wished to say would depend on the other's discerning eye. Such a work—immaculate, but certainly not innocent—would be empty enough and sufficiently generous to satisfy every expectation and to exceed anything I myself might have been capable of imagining while inventing this series of ineffectual little tales.

From the very outset, the project I had in mind involved the writing of a LIBER MUTUS—that "silent book" whose mysterious and vacant meaning was the only grail that ever seemed worthy of my pursuit, that unknown book that offers its pages wide open to whomever might want to approach them without losing courage, without averting their eyes from the dizzying surface where nothing lies written prior to the moment of its reading. A foolhardy project, of course, based as it is on the dream of a virgin book whose inviolate text would be released only by the act of reading and whose resultant lines and paragraphs would follow the movements of a thought process until then held captive, its pages animated only by the generous gaze of a reader prepared to see in them what no one before had suspected.

This book is very ancient—and very modern. As it makes its way ashore, it creates flecks of black-and-white foam (distant cries from the past, veiled allusions to archaic practices of kissing, of killing, of saying farewell). It advances with the whole wave swell of this past bearing it forward, its breakers rolling in with the collective crash of forgotten lives, resounding with all that is alive and joyous, all that is tragic or inopportune—the roar of the hosts of the dead, their persistent customs, their frivolous ways, their abandoned rituals, their deposed sovereigns, their trails of tears, their words of love echoing on long after their bodies have disappeared.

The author-reader-witness-hero of this book invests its words with the power to speak for all time, unwilling to shy away from what the future promises or from the eventual circumstances of their own death. This absolute knowledge lies beyond reach, for the presumptuous reader would have to agree to read the same blank pages over and over without exhausting their emptiness; the reader would have to submit to the risk of a reading that was different on each occasion, until the reader's existence became one with the vanity of the book, which, ceasing at that point to provide satisfaction, would precipitate the reader's fall.

The reader's eyes will grow weary; the reader will dread this book that is without end and that bears no title. The tale, thought out and unfolded in the mind of the ideal reader, now slips away. The reader's eyes henceforth find themselves facing blank pages, empty except for the occasional bits of crabbed handwriting in the margins—tiny tracks, filled with gaps, like cutoff sentences. ASER . . . *wou* . . . *ang* . . . *liv* . . . Thus translated by the reader:

> *ASEROË wounded angel lives.*

Before the book apparently comes to a close—and it's a big book, judging by the thickness of the volume, made up as it is of so many blank pages (or "beauties," as the typographers call them)—a torn sheet emerges from its depths, of which only a lateral fragment remains, featuring an inner margin on which the words *ang* . . . and

liv ... are inscribed, as well as further phrases
that nobody has signed.

We see this tear sheet, far older than the book
that contains it. We hear laughter, cries, weeping, all these noises then sucked up by silence
and scattered this way and that, like seeds
strewn on the cold, desolate ground. There, in
the night of the dead, lie models without portraits, the folly of forgotten promises, and the
errant words that now and then remind us of the
early sorrows of little children.

12

Aseroë

W HAT IS THE VOCATION of the dead? This crazy, answerless question would be the fruit of the ordeal that I first imposed on myself upon discovering this fragment from *The Testament* of Orpheus:

> THOU SHALT FIND A SPRING TO
> THE LEFT AND A WHITE CYPRESS.
> TAKE CARE NOT TO APPROACH
> THIS SPRING. THOU SHALT FIND
> ANOTHER FROM WHENCE FLOW
> THE COOL WATERS OF THE LAKE
> OF MEMORY. BEFORE IT STAND THE
> GUARDIANS. AND THOU SHALT SAY
> UNTO THEM . . .

From the first time I read this, I vowed to explore the path toward the Other Language, to discover the instructions, the passwords without which Orpheus could not have spoken to the guardians of the forbidden threshold. To bestow life upon the ellipses following the words SAY UNTO THEM, to pass through the portal without loss of life or voice—such, from the very outset, was my dearest wish. In short, to become as Orpheus, to obtain that special dispensation that would allow me to pass through life into death, singing. And what's more, I nurtured the insane hope that upon my return journey, I would not yield to the blackmail of the lament that trailed behind me. I would not turn around before I had reached broad daylight. I would carry the Unknown Language back with me.

However mad my ambitions, I wasn't oblivious to the dire consequences of such a project—to whose repeated failures the bemused disdain of my contemporaries could certainly be added. But what did it matter? I was not dealing with maenads. To experience failure and disdain was a small price to pay for the adventure that awaited me.

But there was a more serious objection that came to mind: "The gods are unfamiliar to you;

you wouldn't even know how to begin to invoke their favor." And what about the inevitable likelihood that I would entirely forget everything I had seen beyond the forbidden threshold, once I returned safe and sound? And the nagging question: "Why hurl yourself into the abyss? There will be ample occasion for that when it comes to be your turn."

Every day I would examine my blank sheet of paper, then gaze at the horizon. I scanned the faces I knew; I spied on others unknown to me. I awaited messages that might be arriving from elsewhere; I awaited a special herald bearing a sign that might arise from daily events; I awaited a lover's secret. There was nothing: I could discover no special indication that my expectations might be fulfilled. The words that followed the THOU SHALT SAY in *The Testament* of Orpheus refused to appear. The ellipses remained: THE COOL WATERS OF THE LAKE OF MEMORY. . . . THE GUARDIANS. . . . THOU SHALT SAY . . . To say, to sing, to scream out—yes—but for whom or what? Innocence is no longer permitted once memory is involved: to refuse forgetfulness is, by the same token, to restore the stifled cries of all those millions of senseless lives whose names are now gone. Is their list on file somewhere? If so, what echo can reach back through all this irreparable distress? At most it might produce the whisper of numberless victims, a murmur of all those legions who lie discarded. And who was I to imagine myself frolicking about in happy song, playing at being inspired by logos and lyre? Once I had passed over the threshold, the song I would discover would not be divine: it would merely be the song of unheard screams, of silence.

Furthermore, whose orders was I supposed to obey in order to make any real progress? Or should I just fall silent, lest I fail? The more I reread the fragment, the more I felt myself drawn to the Other Language. I needed to respond, even though there might be no promise of an answer.

Sometimes I imagine that, in the absence of any response, all one can do is remain alone and wait. This waiting must be so prolonged that no sentence could ever fill in its ellipses. At which point it's just possible that a reader might fall in love with Orpheus's unfinished command and might add his or her expectations to mine, in turn stimulating other readers to respond without ever closing the cycle of questions. Thus, question after question might echo forth, all spiraling around the same enigma, caught up in the undecidable movement of the Unknown Language, ever reaching forward.

Every morning, I observe the daylight. It fills us with talk; it bears us onward. I watch the children playing around the lake; I notice the bent-over figures of the old people strolling through parks; I see three young idiots on *green motorcycles* plowing their way through a mound of greenery covered with anemones. The sheer joys of the present moment are enough to make one forget all one's troubles. The ordinary words of the world come to us in broad daylight like the flames of Pentecost descending upon the heads of the apostles and it seems as if we miraculously speak in tongues. But as the daylight wanes, the ellipses of the unfinished sentence come back to me and pursue me through the dark. There I wait and listen, gritting my teeth in order not to reveal my anger and frustration. Sometimes, my vigilance weakens and I yield to the cowardice of sleep—just as soldiers are said to doze off toward dawn after having kept vigil all night long while awaiting the onset of the morning battle.

Ideally, I would have nothing to say or do. I would simply give myself over to whatever came along or to whatever sentences I might hear, even the most ordinary ones: "Go fetch some bread", "The children are coming over this evening", "Someone's at the door, let me get it." This is where the answers I seek will emerge, from the accumulation of phrases, from the accretion of inert objects that bear within themselves—like the faint sorrow on the face of a young girl—the trace of lost voices. I would learn to read the air, to decode the vibrations it transmits. I would learn how to decipher the cracks in tortoise shells or the marks on charred bones, in the manner of the ancient Chinese. I would rediscover a state of the world prior to the separation of names from things. I would learn the art of "the rectification of names" (*chêng ming*). I would learn forms of writing that had not been invented but that inhered in our perception of the world.

I discovered this morning, sitting on my windowsill, a stone that I had brought back from the Alps of Savoy—a piece of quartz that contains within it those even finer dark red crystals commonly called "love arrows" or "Venus hair." Seen from a certain angle, the crystals form a denser structure, a double sign whose patterning I'll try to trace on this white sheet of paper:

This is the ideogram of Tao. The radical to the left 辵 means "to drift," which in turn derives from 彳亍, "to proceed slowly step by step," a character that reaches back to 行, which represents a road. The component to the right comes from "the head, someone in the act of looking" 首. Combined, the two portions of the ideogram evoke the following event: "Someone slowly advances step by step, then stops to look, before proceeding. . . ."

Astonished by my discovery, I believed I had finally discovered the Writing from Without that answered all my expectations. I ran back to my village and, notebook in hand, made my way along the path that started at the river. I counted to thirteen, hoping to discover further marvels. The first one, Kruger's red house, not far from my own. Second, the list of names and addresses that Jean-Michel had placed in my mailbox. Third, a light clump of feathers beneath a gutter sheltering a pair of wood pigeons. Fourth, a linen sheet and a pair of maid's hands on a windowsill. Fifth, a beautiful specimen of *Orchys purpurea*, hidden near the washtub between the nettles and the gravel. Sixth, a hay cart decorated with a goat skull. Seventh, a child's drawing dropped in the gutter near the school. Eighth, a dark garden well choked with weeds. Ninth, a morose old drunk in a bar named The Star. Tenth, a display shelf next to the cash register of the local convenience store stacked with copies of *TV Guides*. Eleventh, a wall displaying a poster of Naïma, a little girl who was kidnapped two years ago and would now be fourteen, sequestered in what den of iniquity? Twelfth, a boy in a yellow sweater emerging from an alleyway holding a bouquet of daffodils. I was so happy, I caught hold of him and took him in my arms, as if our meeting had just rescued me from a grave danger. "Stop, you're hurting me, and besides, you're not my father." And his mother, who came running up: "Leave the kid alone; he didn't do anything to you." Farther on, this other voice: "What time are you boarding?" Car noises, a door slamming. The air smelling of dawn, of boxwood, of kisses.

Between "boxwood" and "kisses," the boy, crumpled on the ground twenty feet away from me, dropped his bouquet of daffodils and got up again, crying and pointing an accusing finger at me: "It's your fault; you made me fall by looking at me." The mother, who had witnessed the entire Orphic mission I sensed myself invested with, shouted out, "You bastard!" I laughed good-naturedly, which she couldn't understand. Then bullfinches flying under a flowering maple tree, executing the perfect loop of a mating

173

dance, spelling out the letters *j* and *a* against the sky—not the initial letters of the French *jamais,* or *jadis,* but the *ja* of a foreign language calling out questions that death could no longer dismiss:

> *Preise dem Engel die Welt, nicht die unsägliche. . . .*

> *Praise the world to the angel, not what's unsayable. . . .*

A Note on this Translation

COMPOSED DURING THE LATE 1980s—when I first became fast friends with its author in Dijon—*Aseroë* was published by the prestigious publishing house of POL in 1992, to excellent reviews. An initial translation of the book was undertaken by Howard Limoli in 1996, but this version was left uncompleted at his death in 2013. Anxious to see his novel in print in English, François Dominique subsequently asked me to rewrite the draft translation of the text, whose original had in the meantime also undergone a number of revisions. This is the version given here: a co-translation by the late Limoli and myself—an Orphic commerce between the living and the dead, which reenacts some of this book's deepest and most enigmatic themes.

—Richard Sieburth

BELLEVUE LITERARY PRESS is devoted to publishing
literary fiction and nonfiction at the intersection of
the arts and sciences because we believe that science
and the humanities are natural companions for
understanding the human experience. With each book
we publish, our goal is to foster a rich, interdisciplinary
dialogue that will forge new tools for thinking and
engaging with the world.

To support our press and its mission,
and for our full catalogue of published titles,
please visit us at blpress.org.

BELLEVUE LITERARY PRESS
New York